"THE DIVINE GUARDIANS: THE TEMPLE OF TEN DOORS"

PART ONE

PSS PRANAV

ॐ त्र्यम्बकं यजामहे सुगन्धिं पुष्टिवर्धनम् ।
उर्वारुकमिव बन्धनान्मृत्योर्मुक्षीय माऽमृतात् ॥

[We worship the Three-eyed Lord who is fragrant and who nourishes and nurtures all beings. As is the ripened cucumber is freed from its bondage, may He liberate us from death for the sake of immortality.']

To the countless heroes and heroines, both real and imagined, who inspire us to be brave, kind, and resilient. May your stories continue to light our paths. **OM NAMAH SHIVAYA**.

Contents

Contents

Foreword

"**B**EFORE YOU READ THIS NOVEL.

A boy named Shiva and his friends embark on an extraordinary adventure together. What starts as a simple trip transforms into a thrilling journey filled with ancient mysteries, mythical powers, and deep friendships. As they encounter challenges that test their courage and unity, they uncover secrets that link them to the gods themselves, setting them on a path to becoming heroes. With each step, Shiva and his friends learn that their destiny is far greater than they ever imagined, and their bond is the key to overcoming the forces of darkness.

CHARACTER BIO DATA:-

Shiva

1. Appearance: Tall and athletic with sharp features, usually calm and composed.

2. Personality: Wise and meditative, with a deep sense of responsibility and balance.

3. Divine Form: Transforms into Lord Shiva, the destroyer and restorer of worlds.

4. Abilities: Master of cosmic energy, wielding a powerful trident (Trishula) and capable of immense destruction and regeneration.

5. Role: Often the group's leader and strategist, providing guidance and wisdom.

6. Strengths: Unyielding resolve, deep insight, and profound spiritual knowledge.

7. Weaknesses: Can be overly cautious and contemplative, sometimes slow to action.

8. Background: Raised in a traditional household with a strong emphasis on spiritual practices.

9. Relationships: Respected and trusted by all team members,

often a mentor figure.

10. Motivation: Dedicated to maintaining cosmic balance and protecting the world from evil.

Krishna

1. Appearance: Charming and charismatic, with a playful smile and twinkling eyes.

2. Personality: Mischievous, witty, and extremely intelligent, with a penchant for diplomacy.

3. Divine Form: Transforms into Lord Krishna, the supreme strategist and diplomat.

4. Abilities: Master of illusion (Maya), expert in music with his divine flute, and skilled in combat.

5. Role: The group's strategist and morale booster, often diffusing tense situations with his wit.

6. Strengths: Exceptional problem-solving skills, charm, and the ability to inspire and lead.

7. Weaknesses: His playful nature can sometimes be misunderstood as lack of seriousness.

8. Background: Grew up learning various arts and sciences, with a deep understanding of human nature.

9. Relationships: Close friend to all, especially Arjuna, with whom he shares a deep bond.

10. Motivation: To bring about righteousness and protect his loved ones from harm.

Ram

1. Appearance: Noble and dignified, with a calm and reassuring presence.

2. Personality: Dutiful, honorable, and a natural leader with a strong sense of justice.

3. Divine Form: Transforms into Lord Ram, the epitome of virtue and righteousness.

4. Abilities: Master archer, unparalleled in combat skills, and a paragon of dharma.

5. Role: The group's moral compass and primary warrior, often leading from the front.

6. Strengths: Unwavering sense of duty, exceptional combat skills, and leadership qualities.

7. Weaknesses: His strict adherence to duty can sometimes make him inflexible.

8. Background: Raised in a royal family, with rigorous training in statecraft and combat.

9. Relationships: Deeply respects and cares for Lakshman, his loyal companion and brother.

10. Motivation: To uphold righteousness and protect his people from evil.

Anju (Hanuman)

1. Appearance: Energetic and muscular, with a vibrant and dynamic presence.

2. Personality: Loyal, courageous, and always eager to help, with a childlike enthusiasm.

3. Divine Form: Transforms into Lord Hanuman, the mighty monkey god.

4. Abilities: Immense strength, the ability to fly, and unparalleled devotion and bravery.

5. Role: The group's powerhouse and scout, often taking on physically demanding tasks.

6. Strengths: Boundless energy, unwavering loyalty, and extraordinary physical prowess.

7. Weaknesses: His enthusiasm can sometimes lead to impulsiveness.

8. Background: Comes from a humble background, with a strong sense of duty and devotion.

9. Relationships: Shares a deep bond with Ram, whom he serves with absolute loyalty.

10. Motivation: Driven by devotion and the desire to protect his friends and uphold justice.

Lakshman

1. Appearance: Athletic and vigilant, with an intense and focused demeanor.

2. Personality: Devoted, protective, and fiercely loyal, often acting as the group's guardian.

3. Divine Form: Transforms into Lord Lakshman, the devoted brother and warrior.

4. Abilities: Exceptional swordsmanship, unyielding determination, and protective instincts.

5. Role: The group's protector and second-in-command, always ready to defend his companions.

6. Strengths: Steadfast loyalty, combat expertise, and a strong sense of duty.

7. Weaknesses: His protective nature can sometimes make him overbearing.

8. Background: Raised alongside Ram, with rigorous training in combat and statecraft.

9. Relationships: Deeply bonded with Ram, serving as his loyal companion and protector.

10. Motivation: To protect his brother and uphold the principles of righteousness.

Saraswati

1. Appearance: Graceful and serene, with an aura of wisdom and tranquility.

2. Personality: Wise, calm, and nurturing, with a profound understanding of knowledge and art.

3. Divine Form: Transforms into Goddess Saraswati, the deity of wisdom and learning.

4. Abilities: Mastery of knowledge, arts, and music, with the power to inspire and enlighten.

5. Role: The group's source of wisdom and strategic guidance, often providing insights and solutions.

6. Strengths: Vast knowledge, calm demeanor, and the ability to inspire creativity and learning.

7. Weaknesses: Her calm nature can sometimes be mistaken for passivity.

8. Background: Grew up in an environment rich in learning and culture, with a deep love for the arts.

9. Relationships: Respected by all, often seen as a mentor and guide.

10. Motivation: To spread wisdom and knowledge, and to help her friends achieve their goals.

Arjuna

1. Appearance: Tall and athletic, with sharp features and intense eyes.

2. Personality: Competitive, determined, and highly skilled, with a strong sense of duty.

3. Divine Form: Transforms into Arjuna, the peerless archer and hero of the Mahabharata.

4. Abilities: Exceptional archery skills, strategic mind, and warrior prowess.

5. Role: The group's primary archer and tactician, often taking the lead in combat scenarios.

6. Strengths: Unmatched archery skills, strategic thinking, and a strong moral compass.

7. Weaknesses: His competitive nature can sometimes lead to conflicts.

8. Background: Raised as a prince, with extensive training in warfare and strategy.

9. Relationships: Shares a deep bond with Krishna, who often guides him.

10. Motivation: To uphold dharma and prove himself as the greatest warrior.

Karna

1. Appearance: Strong and imposing, with a regal and determined demeanor.

2. Personality: Noble, resilient, and driven by a desire to prove his worth.

3. Divine Form: Transforms into Karna, the formidable warrior and son of the Sun God.

4. Abilities: Exceptional combat skills, impenetrable armor, and immense strength.

5. Role: The group's warrior and rival to Arjuna, providing balance and challenge.

6. Strengths: Unyielding determination, combat prowess, and a strong sense of honor.

7. Weaknesses: His pride and desire to prove himself can sometimes cloud his judgment.

8. Background: Raised in humble circumstances, with a burning desire to rise above his station.

9. Relationships: Respectful rivalry with Arjuna, with whom he shares a complex bond.

10. Motivation: To prove his worth and honor, and to protect those he cares about.

Character Sketch: Abhi

Name: Abhi

Appearance: Abhi is a lean yet muscular young man with an athletic build that hints at his exceptional physical abilities. He has dark, tousled hair that often falls over his intense, observant eyes. His calm and composed demeanor can make him appear somewhat aloof, but there's an undeniable aura of strength and confidence around him. His posture and movements are fluid and graceful, reminiscent of a tiger, reflecting his unique ability.

Personality: Abhi is initially perceived as an introvert, preferring solitude over social interaction. He is quiet and reserved, often found engrossed in his studies or deep in thought. Despite his quiet nature, he possesses a keen intellect and a sharp observational skill, making him highly perceptive and aware of his surroundings. Abhi is introspective and thoughtful, always analyzing situations and people around him.

Abilities: Abhi has the extraordinary ability to transform his physique and fighting style to resemble that of a tiger. This unique power grants him enhanced agility, strength, and reflexes, making him a formidable fighter. His movements are swift and precise, embodying the grace and power of the majestic animal he channels. This ability, however, is kept hidden from most, revealing itself only to those he trusts.

Background: Abhi's background is shrouded in mystery, adding to his enigmatic presence. He has always been cautious about revealing his abilities, fearing judgment and misunderstanding. His past experiences have made him wary of forming close relationships, leading to his initial solitude. However, beneath this guarded exterior lies a deep longing for acceptance and belonging.

Interests: Abhi has a profound interest in history and mythology, often spending hours reading ancient texts and scriptures. His love for knowledge extends to various subjects, making him well-versed and knowledgeable. He also has a keen interest in martial arts, which complements his tiger-like fighting style.

Strengths: Abhi's greatest strengths lie in his physical prowess and intellectual capabilities. His ability to channel the strength and agility of a tiger makes him a powerful ally in combat. Additionally, his sharp mind and perceptive nature enable him to analyze and strategize effectively. His calm demeanor under pressure and his ability to remain focused and composed are invaluable assets.

Weaknesses: Abhi's reserved nature can sometimes make it difficult for him to connect with others, leading to feelings of isolation. His tendency to keep his abilities and true self hidden can create barriers between him and those around him. Additionally, his cautiousness can sometimes be mistaken for aloofness, making it challenging for others to understand and get close to him.

Development: Over time, Abhi begins to open up and form bonds with the group of friends he joins. Their acceptance and camaraderie help him overcome his fears and embrace his true self. As he becomes more comfortable sharing his abilities, he discovers the strength that comes from unity and friendship. Abhi's journey is one of self-discovery and acceptance, learning to balance his solitary nature with the joys of companionship and trust."

Preface

In a world where ancient myths intertwine with the present, ordinary lives can be touched by the extraordinary. This is the story of Shiva and his friends—six ordinary boys whose lives are forever changed when they stumble upon powers rooted in the legends of gods and demons.

What begins as a routine school trip soon spirals into an epic adventure, one that takes them from the familiar surroundings of their everyday world to the mysterious depths of ancient temples, enchanted forests, and beyond. Along the way, they discover that they are more than mere students—they are the bearers of divine legacies, entrusted with protecting the world from a long-dormant evil that has begun to stir once more.

This tale is about friendship, bravery, and the discovery of inner strength. It is a journey of self-discovery, as each boy learns that the key to their power lies not only in the gods they channel but also in the unbreakable bond they share with one another. Together, they will face trials and battles that test their limits, but through it all, their unity and determination will forge them into heroes.

In these pages, the lines between myth and reality blur, and the adventure of a lifetime begins. This is their story—a story of courage, loyalty, and the awakening of ancient power.

Welcome to *The Chronicles of the Ancient Warriors*.

Acknowledgements

This book would not have been possible without the support and encouragement of many individuals.

First and foremost, I would like to thank my family,my mother, my father and my little sister, whose love and support have been my anchor. To my friends, who have been my sounding board and my biggest cheerleaders – your unwavering belief in me has been invaluable.

A heartfelt thank you to my editor, whose keen eye and thoughtful suggestions have greatly improved this manuscript. To my publisher, for believing in this story and helping bring it to life.

I am also grateful to the countless storytellers, both ancient and contemporary, whose works have inspired me and whose stories continue to ignite my imagination.

Lastly, to the readers – thank you for embarking on this journey with me. Your support and enthusiasm mean the world to me.

Prologue

In a time long past, the gods walked among mortals, their presence a beacon of hope and strength. These divine beings, with their extraordinary powers and boundless wisdom, guided humanity through trials and tribulations, teaching them the virtues of courage, compassion, and unity.

But as the ages turned and the world evolved, the gods retreated to their celestial abodes, leaving behind a world where their influence was felt but their presence unseen. In this modern age, the essence of the divine still lingers, manifesting in ways unexpected and profound.

In the bustling city of Hyderabad, a group of extraordinary children discovered that the gods had not entirely departed. Shiva, Krishna, Ram, Anju, Lakshman, and Saraswati – each with the unique ability to transform into the gods of old – found themselves tasked with a mission that transcended time. Alongside their friends Arjuna and Karna, they navigated the challenges of both the mortal and divine realms, their bond forged in the fires of battle and the celebrations of life.

Their journey took them from the mysterious temple where they faced the formidable Kaal to the vibrant streets of Hyderabad, where they reveled in the joy of festivals and the strength of their unity. Through their adventures, they learned that the true power of the gods lay not in their extraordinary abilities but in their unwavering faith in each other.

This is their story – a tale of gods and mortals, of ancient legends and modern heroes, of battles fought and celebrations shared. As they face the trials ahead, they remind us that the spirit of the divine lives on in each of us, guiding us through the darkness and illuminating our path with the light of friendship and love.

About The Author

PSS Pranav is an avid storyteller with a deep passion for fictional narratives and a profound appreciation for the vibrant world of anime. His love for storytelling is matched only by his enthusiasm for cricket, a sport that brings him immense joy and satisfaction. Pranav's respect for tradition and his reverence for elders are integral parts of his character, reflecting his values and principles.

A student of life and literature, Pranav's curiosity extends beyond contemporary fiction and anime. He has a keen interest in Hindu scriptures and philosophy, which deeply influences his writing. His exploration of these ancient texts enriches his understanding of cultural and spiritual themes, weaving them into his stories in a way that honors tradition while engaging modern readers.

In his writing, Pranav combines his diverse interests to create narratives that are not only entertaining but also thought-provoking. His characters and plots often reflect the values he holds dear—respect for wisdom, the pursuit of knowledge, and the joy of discovery. Through his work, Pranav invites readers to embark on adventures that blend the magical with the meaningful, the imaginative with the introspective.

When he is not writing, Pranav can often be found on the cricket field, engaging in spirited matches, or immersed in his favorite anime series, exploring new realms of imagination and excitement. His stories are a testament to his vibrant personality and his commitment to blending the best of fiction with profound, real-world insights.

Keywords and Their Meanings:
1. Adventure - A daring and exciting experience or journey, often involving exploration.
2. Awe - A feeling of reverential respect mixed with fear or wonder.
3. Bean Bags - Soft, cushioned seating often used for comfort and relaxation.
4. Birthday - The anniversary of the day on which a person was born.
5. Blush - To become red in the face due to embarrassment or modesty.
6. Camaraderie - A spirit of friendship and community among a group.
7. Chemistry - The branch of science that deals with the composition, properties, and reactions of substances.
8. Credits - The list of names of those who contributed to a film, shown at the end of the movie.
9. Curiosity - A strong desire to learn or know something.
10. Eerie - Strange and frightening, often causing unease.
11. Enthusiasm - Intense and eager enjoyment or interest.
12. Fascinated - Extremely interested or captivated by something.
13. Fear - An unpleasant emotion caused by the belief that someone or something is dangerous.
14. Festival - A series of events or performances celebrating a particular aspect of culture.
15. Glimpse - A brief or fleeting view or sight.
16. Gratitude - The quality of being thankful; readiness to show appreciation.
17. Heartfelt - Deeply and sincerely felt or expressed.
18. Intrigue - The quality of arousing curiosity or interest.
19. Journey - An act of traveling from one place to another, often with personal growth.
20. Keystone - The central, supportive element of something, often

used metaphorically.

21. Legend - A traditional story or myth handed down through generations.

22. Lively - Full of energy and activity; animated.

23. Mythology - A collection of myths or stories from a particular culture or religion.

24. Narrative - A spoken or written account of connected events; a story.

25. Presence - The state or fact of existing or being present.

26. Reverence - Deep respect or admiration.

27. Sensory - Relating to the senses or sensations.

28. Serene - Calm, peaceful, and untroubled.

29. Shadowy - Dark or obscure, often associated with mystery.

30. Shared - Something that is used or experienced by multiple people.

31. Special - Distinct from what is ordinary; unique or particularly valued.

32. Spiritual - Relating to the soul or spirit, often associated with religion.

33. Storytelling - The act of narrating stories or events.

34. Triumph - A great victory or achievement.

35. Unsettling - Causing anxiety or discomfort; disturbing.

36. Voyage - A long journey, especially by sea or in space.

37. Warmth - The quality of being warm and comforting; a sense of coziness.

38. Wisdom - The ability to make sound judgments and decisions based on knowledge and experience.

39. Zeal - Great energy or enthusiasm in pursuit of a cause or objective.

40. Awakening - The act of becoming aware of something; a realization.

41. Cultural - Relating to the ideas, customs, and social behavior of a society.

42. Dialogue - A conversation or discussion between two or more people.

43. Dynamic - Characterized by constant change or activity.

44. Engagement - Participation or involvement in an activity or event.

45. Exhilaration - A feeling of excitement and happiness.

46. Festival - A series of organized events celebrating a particular aspect of culture.

47. Harmony - The state of being in agreement or concord; balance.

48. Immersion - Deep involvement or engagement in a particular activity or subject.

49. Inspiration - The process of being mentally stimulated to do something creative.

50. Interaction - Communication or direct involvement with someone or something.

51. Jubilant - Feeling or expressing great happiness and triumph.

52. Legacy - Something handed down by predecessors, often a lasting impact or memory.

53. Mythical - Relating to myths or mythical beings; often supernatural or legendary.

54. Narrative - The structured account of connected events or stories.

55. Occasion - A particular event or instance that is noteworthy.

56. Paradox - A statement or situation that contradicts itself but may reveal a truth.

57. Revelation - A surprising and previously unknown fact that has been disclosed.

58. Sacred - Regarded with reverence and respect, often in a religious context.

59. Serendipity - The occurrence of events by chance in a happy or beneficial way.

60. Spectacle - A visually striking performance or display.

61. Symbolic - Serving as a symbol or representation of something else.

62. Tension - Mental or emotional strain, or suspense in a narrative.

63. Unity - The state of being united or joined as a whole.

64. Vivid - Producing powerful feelings or strong, clear images in the

mind.

65. Whimsy - Playfulness or quaintness, often characterized by fanciful or amusing behavior.

66. Zephyr - A gentle, mild breeze; used metaphorically to signify a light, pleasant feeling.

67. Awareness - The state of being conscious of something.

68. Bond - A connection or relationship between people or elements.

69. Curiosity - A desire to learn or know more about something.

70. Discovery - The act of finding or learning something new.

71. Epic - A long, narrative poem or story detailing heroic deeds or adventures.

72. Festivity - The celebration or enjoyment of a festival.

73. Gratification - Satisfaction or pleasure derived from something achieved or experienced.

74. Harmony - Agreement or concord; often used to describe balanced and pleasing combinations.

75. Incredible - Difficult to believe; extraordinary.

76. Journey - A long and often adventurous trip or voyage.

77. Kaleidoscope - A constantly changing pattern or sequence of events.

78. Luminescence - The emission of light by a substance not resulting from heat.

79. Myth - A traditional story or belief that explains natural phenomena or customs.

80. Nostalgia - A sentimental longing for the past.

81. Odyssey - A long, adventurous journey or quest.

82. Perspective - A particular attitude or way of considering something.

83. Quest - A long or arduous search for something.

84. Reverie - A state of being pleasantly lost in one's thoughts; daydreaming.

85. Saga - A long, involved story or series of incidents.

86. Tapestry - A complex and intricate combination of things, often used metaphorically.

87. Universe - All existing matter and space considered as a whole.

88. Visionary - Having or showing clear ideas about what should happen or be done.

89. Whimsy - The quality of being playful and imaginative.

90. Xenial - Relating to hospitality and friendliness towards guests.

91. Yearning - A deep, often melancholic longing or desire.

92. Zenith - The highest point or peak of something, often used metaphorically.

93. Ambiance - The character and atmosphere of a place.

94. Banter - Light, playful, and friendly exchange of remarks.

95. Celestial - Pertaining to the sky or heavens; heavenly.

96. Dramatic - Relating to drama; filled with excitement or emotion.

97. Elation - Great happiness or joy.

98. Fable - A short story with a moral lesson, often featuring animals as characters.

99. Glimmer - A faint or wavering light or hope.

100. Holographic - Relating to holography; a method of producing three-dimensional images.

These keywords and their meanings reflect the rich tapestry of elements woven into the story, capturing the essence of its adventures, characters, and themes.

1

Chapter 1: The INTRODUCTION

A boy named Shiva had recently shifted to Hyderabad. His father was a businessman and his mother was a housewife. He recently got admission for'**Shree rishi international school'**. He liked how everyone greeted him.Krishna a boy, in the same class as Shiva, greeted him and took him to their class, and introduced him to his friends, they were Anji, Ram, Lucky.Krishna said, "you're so lucky, we are going on an excursion to a temple in Kerala in one month". "oh!" shiva exclaimed with joy. Krishna and everyone told what was going on in class and gave their notes to shiva.

Shiva felt a rush of excitement at the prospect of the upcoming trip. As the days passed, he quickly settled into his new routine at Shree Rishi International School. The school was vast and had all the modern amenities, but what Shiva liked the most was the friendliness of his classmates.

During lunch breaks, Shiva and his new friends, Krishna, Anji, Ram, and Lucky, would gather under a large banyan tree in the school courtyard. They shared stories, jokes, and snacks, bonding over their shared experiences and interests. Shiva felt grateful for their warm welcome.

One day, Krishna mentioned the temple they would be visiting in Kerala. "It's called the Padmanabhaswamy Temple," he explained.

"It's one of the richest and most mysterious temples in the world. There are legends of hidden treasures and secret chambers."

Shiva's curiosity was piqued. "Hidden treasures? That sounds fascinating! Do you think we'll get to see any of it?"

Lucky laughed. "I doubt it! But the temple is beautiful, and the journey will be an adventure."

2

Krishna's village

Krishna invited Shiva to his village for the Sankranti festival, which brought a three-day holiday from school. Shiva, having no other plans, asked his parents for permission. They agreed, and soon Shiva and Krishna, accompanied by Krishna's parents, set off on a train journey to the village of Amalapuram. They arrived the next day, and after freshening up and enjoying a hearty lunch, they spent the afternoon playing games until they were thoroughly tired.

Seeking some rest, they sat under a majestic 150-year-old tree. Shiva, curious about Krishna's talents, asked, "Do you know how to play any musical instruments?"

"Yes, I can play the flute," Krishna replied with a smile. He dashed inside his house and returned with a briefcase containing two flutes.

Shiva, puzzled, asked, "Why are you carrying two flutes?"

Krishna explained, "In case one breaks, we have a backup. Flutes can be expensive to replace."

"Ah, I see," Shiva said, understanding. Krishna then began to play the flute, filling the air with its melodious tunes.

krishna playing flute

Krishna's flute-playing had created a magical atmosphere under the ancient tree. Small sparrows fluttered around, cows grazed peacefully nearby, butterflies danced in the air, and even a few deer emerged from the surrounding woods, drawn by the melodious tunes. Shiva, lulled by the serene music, had drifted into a peaceful nap.

Krishna's fingers moved skillfully over the flute, producing sweet, harmonious notes. However, after a while, he began to tire and his energy waned. He stopped playing, taking deep breaths to regain his strength. The music ceased, and the animals gradually dispersed, returning to their natural activities.

Shiva stirred and opened his eyes, feeling remarkably refreshed. "That was the best five minutes of sleep I've ever had," he said, stretching and yawning.

Krishna smiled. "The power of music, my friend. It has a way of soothing the soul."

The rest of their time in Amalapuram was filled with joyous activities. They explored the village, visited Krishna's relatives, and took part in the Sankranti festivities. They flew colorful kites, participated in traditional games, and enjoyed delicious festive foods. Shiva was fascinated by the customs and traditions, and he felt deeply connected to the rich culture of the village.

One memorable evening, they joined the villagers in a bonfire celebration. As the flames crackled and danced, people sang folk songs and shared stories. Krishna's flute once again became the centerpiece, enchanting everyone with its melodious tunes. Shiva couldn't help but feel a sense of wonder and joy as he watched his friend play under the starry sky.

The three days flew by, and soon it was time to return to Hyderabad. Shiva bid farewell to Krishna's family and the village, carrying with him fond memories of the Sankranti festival and the warmth of the villagers. The train journey back was filled with conversations about their experiences, and Shiva realized how much he had grown to appreciate the simple yet profound beauty of village life.

Back in school, life resumed its usual pace. Classes, assignments, and extracurricular activities kept everyone busy. Shiva, Krishna, Anji, Ram, and Lucky continued to bond over their shared interests. The group often reminisced about their trips, and Shiva would eagerly share his experiences from Amalapuram, making his friends envious of the village's charm.

One month passed in a blur of schoolwork and fun. Then, one day, as they were sitting under the banyan tree during lunch, Krishna had an idea. "Why don't we start a music club? We can share our love for music and maybe even learn new instruments."

Shiva's eyes lit up. "That's a great idea! I've always wanted to learn the flute. And we can invite others to join us too."

Ram nodded enthusiastically. "Count me in. I'd love to learn the drums."

Lucky grinned. "I can play the guitar. This could be really fun!"

The friends approached their teacher with the idea, and with her support, they started the music club. They met after school and on weekends, experimenting with different instruments and learning from each other. Krishna taught Shiva the basics of the flute, while Lucky showed Ram how to play the drums. The club grew as more students joined, bringing their own instruments and talents.

The music club became a vibrant part of the school community. They performed at school events, festivals, and even organized small concerts. Shiva found immense joy in playing the flute, and he often thought back to that magical afternoon under the old tree in Amalapuram. It was there that his love for music had truly blossomed.

As the month's passed, the friends grew closer, united by their shared passion for music. They supported each other through challenges, celebrated their successes, and created lasting memories. Shiva felt grateful for the journey that had begun with a simple invitation to a village, leading to friendships and experiences that enriched his life in countless ways.

ONE MONTH PASSED

3

"The Excursion"

As the day of the trip approached, the excitement among the students reached a fever pitch. Everyone was busy packing and making last-minute preparations. Shiva, Krishna, Anji, Ram, and Lucky could hardly contain their anticipation.

On the morning of the journey, they gathered at the railway station, accompanied by their teachers and a few parent chaperones. The platform buzzed with chatter and laughter as they waited for the bus to arrive. Shiva, carrying his backpack, turned to their teacher, Mrs. Rao, and asked, "Which temple are we going to again?"

Mrs. Rao smiled warmly. "We are going to the Padmanabhaswamy Temple in Kerala. It's an extraordinary place with a rich history."

The bus ride was long but enjoyable. They spent the day playing games, sharing stories, and admiring the changing landscapes outside the windows. They ate packed lunches and snacks, and as night fell, the bus gently rocked them to sleep.

After a journey of one day and twelve hours, they finally arrived in Kerala. The air was filled with the fragrance of blooming flowers and the sound of chirping birds. The lush greenery and serene backwaters greeted them as they stepped off the bus. They traveled by bus to their accommodation, a charming guesthouse near the temple.

The students quickly got freshened up and were served a warm glass of milk each, which helped to refresh them after the long journey. Their excitement was palpable as they gathered their belongings and prepared to visit the temple.

As they approached the Padmanabhaswamy Temple, they were struck by its grandeur. The towering gopuram, intricately carved with scenes from Hindu mythology, loomed majestically against the sky. The temple was surrounded by lush gardens and a sense of tranquility.

Mrs. Rao led them through the grand entrance. "Remember, this is a sacred place. Please show respect and follow the rules."

The students, dressed in traditional attire as required, stepped inside the vast temple complex. They marveled at the exquisite architecture, the detailed carvings, and the sheer scale of the temple. The atmosphere was serene, with the soft chanting of prayers and the scent of incense in the air.

Inside the temple, they were guided through various sections. They saw the sanctum sanctorum, where the deity, Lord Padmanabha, lay in a reclining posture on the serpent Anantha. The deity was adorned with precious jewels and flowers, and the sight left everyone in awe.

The guide explained the temple's history and significance, recounting stories of devotion and miracles associated with the deity. "This temple is not only a place of worship but also a treasure trove of cultural heritage," he said.

Shiva and his friends listened intently, absorbing the rich history and spiritual significance of the temple. They felt a deep sense of reverence as they explored the sacred halls and courtyards.

As they moved through the temple, they noticed the intricate murals and frescoes depicting various mythological stories. Krishna pointed out one mural, "Look, that's Lord Vishnu defeating the demon king Hiranyakashipu. My grandfather used to tell me this story."

They visited the temple's various shrines, each dedicated to different deities. The group was particularly fascinated by the mysterious vaults, rumored to contain immense treasures. Although they couldn't see inside, the legends surrounding them added an air of mystique to their visit.

After spending several hours exploring and absorbing the spiritual ambiance, they gathered in the temple courtyard for a moment of reflection. Mrs. Rao asked them to sit in a circle and share their thoughts and feelings about the visit.

Shiva spoke first, "This temple is more than just a beautiful structure. It's a place where history, culture, and spirituality come together. I feel really connected to something greater here."

Krishna nodded, "Playing the flute under that ancient tree in my village was special, but being here, in such a sacred place, is another kind of magic."

Ram and Lucky shared their feelings of awe and respect for the traditions and stories they had learned. Anji expressed her fascination with the architecture and the detailed carvings

Krishna said there is a mystery about a door,that required some mudra. Shiva found something glowing in the dark. He didn't take it seriously as it was in a corner.As they wandered through the temple, marveling at the intricate carvings and offerings, a boy playing nearby accidentally bumped into them, causing them to stumble towards the sealed door. To their astonishment, they fell into the same corner that shiva saw. At a distance, something was glowing again. Krishna tried to lift it but his hands couldn't lift it so everyone lifted it .Krishna said 'it looks like the snake mudra. They searched the door

THE MYSTORICAL DOOR

They found the door. They kept the mudra the door opened with a sudden bang!

"Let's go inside," Shiva said, his eyes gleaming with excitement. The others nodded in agreement, their hearts pounding with anticipation.

Krishna said 'i am first' and he ran inside the door. Unfortunately, the sand and gravel fell into krishna's eyes.Shiva washed Krishna's eyes with water, and everyone kept their legs slowly and held their hands.

Inside, the temple was a labyrinth of stone corridors and grand chambers, adorned with intricate carvings and statues of gods. The air was thick with the scent of incense and the echoes of their footsteps. As they explored, they stumbled upon a hidden chamber, its walls lined with ancient scriptures and artifacts.

In the center of the chamber stood a pedestal with five glowing orbs, each pulsating with a different color. Mesmerized, the boys approached the pedestal, feeling an inexplicable pull towards the orbs.

"These must be special," Krishna whispered, reaching out to touch the blue orb. As soon as his fingers made contact, a surge of energy coursed through his body, and he transformed into Lord Krishna, adorned with a peacock feather crown and holding a flute.

The others followed suit. Shiva touched the white orb, and in a flash, he became Lord Shiva, with his third eye glowing fiercely. Ram touched the green orb, transforming into Lord Ram, with his bow and arrow at the ready. Anji touched the red orb, becoming Lord Hanuman, with immense strength and agility. Finally, Lakshman touched the yellow orb and became Lord Lakshman, armed with his sword.

As the boys marveled at their new forms, a sinister presence began to seep into the chamber. The air grew cold, and shadows danced menacingly along the walls. From the darkest corner of the room emerged a malevolent force, an ancient evil long imprisoned within the temple.

4

KAAAL!!!!

"You have awakened me," the dark entity hissed, its voice echoing with malice. "I am Kaal, the harbinger of destruction. And now, with my freedom, I shall bring about the end of the world."

The boys, now divine warriors, stood firm, their resolve unshaken. "We will not let you destroy our world," Shiva declared, his voice resonating with power.

Kaal laughed, his form shifting and growing, exuding an aura of pure darkness. "Foolish children, you are no match for me."

The battle began, a clash of titanic forces within the sacred temple. Shiva unleashed his trident, channeling divine energy to strike Kaal. Krishna played his flute, enchanting the surroundings and creating illusions to confuse the enemy. Ram fired arrows imbued with celestial power, piercing through the shadows. Anji, with his immense strength, tore through the darkness with his bare hands. Lakshman defended his friends with his sword, parrying Kaal's attacks with unmatched skill.

Despite their efforts, Kaal's power seemed insurmountable. The temple shook with the force of their battle, and the boys began to tire. But they did not waver.

"We must combine our powers," Ram shouted. "Only then can we defeat him".

AVAKENED KAAL

With a collective nod, the divine warriors focused their energies, merging their powers into a single, unstoppable force. A brilliant light filled the chamber, driving away the shadows and enveloping Kaal.

"No!" Kaal screamed, his form disintegrating under the combined might of the gods. "This cannot be!"

With one final burst of light, Kaal was vanquished, his essence dissipating into nothingness. The temple fell silent, the air clearing of the oppressive darkness.

THE VICTORY

The boys, exhausted but victorious, reverted to their human forms. They looked at each other, a sense of accomplishment and relief washing over them.

"We did it," Krishna said, smiling. "We saved the world."

5

"THE HOTEL"

After the intense fight the boys were exhausted.They stepped outside the door of the temple with a sigh of relief.They had closed the door and the mudra was destroyed and broken into a million pieces!. "no one should go in here" said shiva. Their travel manager was looking for them this meantime.

"BOYS WHERE ARE YOU ALL?SHIVA??? KRISHNA ??? FOR GOD'S SAKE ANSWER ME!?.And he saw them lying unconciously on the ground.He gently poured water on them and they woke up suddenly. "AH, where am I?" Anji woke up . All drank some water and shared some *prashad* or *prashadam* to regain their energy. they worshipped Lord Vishnu there and was going to their hotel in the bus.

bus going back to their hotel

Upon reaching the hotel, the group checked in and found themselves assigned to a large room with six individual beds. The room was spacious and comfortable, a welcome sight after the day's excitement. They settled in, each boy claiming a bed and unpacking their belongings.

As the night grew darker, the boys were about to turn in when there was a soft knock at the door. Krishna, curious, went to open it and found a young girl standing there, looking somewhat distressed.

krishna opening the door

"Hi," she said hesitantly. "I'm Saraswati. All the other rooms are taken, and I have nowhere else to stay. Could I possibly sleep here for the night?"

Krishna turned to his friends, who all nodded in agreement. "Of course, you can stay here," Krishna said, smiling warmly. "We have an extra bed."

Saraswati thanked them and stepped into the room, visibly relieved. She set her small bag down on the spare bed and sat down, looking at the boys with gratitude.

"Thank you so much," she said. "I was really worried about where I would sleep tonight."

The boys welcomed her, and after some introductions, everyone settled down for the night. The room was filled with a peaceful silence as they drifted off to sleep, their minds still buzzing with the events of the day.

The next morning, the boys woke up to the sound of birds chirping outside their window. They gathered around a small table in the room, chatting and planning their day. Saraswati, who had been quiet the previous night, seemed more at ease and joined them.

As they were eating breakfast, Saraswati hesitated for a moment before speaking. "I have something to tell you all," she began, her voice steady. "I wasn't completely honest with you last night. I have a secret."

The boys looked at her curiously, encouraging her to continue.

Saraswati took a deep breath. "Just like you all have the power to transform into gods, I have a similar ability. I can transform into the goddess Saraswati."

The boys were stunned, exchanging astonished glances. Krishna was the first to speak. "That's incredible! How did you discover your power?"

Saraswati smiled, a hint of shyness in her expression. "It happened a few years ago. I was meditating near a river, and suddenly I felt this surge of energy. When I opened my eyes, I had transformed into the goddess Saraswati, complete with a veena and a swan by my side."

saraswati's transformation

Shiva leaned forward, intrigued. "Have you ever used your powers to fight against evil?"

Saraswati nodded. "Yes, but I usually keep a low profile. I prefer to use my abilities to help others through knowledge and wisdom rather than engaging in battles."

Ram, always the strategist, saw potential. "With your powers combined with ours, we could be even stronger. If more threats like Kaal emerge, we'll need all the help we can get."

Anji, always enthusiastic, grinned. "Welcome to the team, Saraswati!"

Lakshman added, "We're glad to have you with us."

Saraswati's face lit up with a grateful smile. "Thank you. I'm honored to join you."

As the morning light filled the room, the friends knew they were bound not only by their extraordinary powers but also by a shared destiny. Together, they would protect the world from any evil that dared to threaten it.

And so, their journey continued, now with Saraswati by their side. United by their divine heritage and their unwavering friendship, they faced the future with confidence, ready to confront any challenges that lay ahead.

"Vedic Heritage Inn."

After a fierce battle with Kaal in a mysterious temple, they found themselves journeying to Hyderabad. The battle had left them exhausted and hungry, compelling them to stop at a unique hotel that caught their eye.

This was no ordinary hotel. It was themed around history, filled with artifacts and stories from ancient times. As they entered, the ambiance of the place mesmerized them. The walls were adorned with murals depicting epic battles, divine interventions, and the tales of legendary heroes.

As the group marveled at the surroundings, a commotion broke out near the entrance. Two boys, Arjuna and Karna, were embroiled in a heated argument about who was the best archer. Their voices echoed through the hall, drawing the attention of everyone present.

Shiva stepped forward, his calm demeanor contrasting with the tension in the air. "What seems to be the issue here?" he asked.

Arjuna, a tall boy with sharp eyes, pointed at Karna. "He claims to be the best archer, but we all know that title belongs to me!"

Karna, equally determined, retorted, "Your skills are nothing compared to mine, Arjuna. I am the true master of archery!"

Before the argument could escalate further, Ram intervened. "Fighting among ourselves will solve nothing. Let us find a peaceful resolution."

Little did they know, Arjuna and Karna were no ordinary boys. They too had the power to transform into their divine counterparts. The air around them shimmered as Arjuna transformed into the mighty warrior Arjuna, and Karna became the indomitable Karna.

Saraswati, sensing the potential for chaos, spoke with authority, "We must not let our powers divide us. We are all part of a greater destiny."

Anju, now in his form as Lord Hanuman, nodded. "Let us settle this with a friendly competition, rather than conflict."

The suggestion was met with approval. They decided to test their skills in a series of challenges, each designed to showcase their abilities without causing harm. The hotel, with its vast open grounds and ancient structures, provided the perfect setting.

The first challenge was a test of accuracy. Arjuna and Karna stood side by side, their bows drawn. They released their arrows simultaneously, each hitting their mark with unparalleled precision. The onlookers gasped in awe, witnessing a display of archery that transcended human capability.

Next was a test of strength. Anju, in his Hanuman form, demonstrated his immense power by lifting a massive boulder effortlessly. Karna, not to be outdone, used his divine strength to match Hanuman's feat.

As the challenges continued, it became clear that both Arjuna and Karna were equally skilled, each excelling in different aspects of their abilities. The rivalry that had threatened to divide them began to transform into mutual respect.

Krishna, with his wisdom and charm, addressed the group. "We are all gifted with extraordinary powers. Instead of competing, let us unite and use our strengths to make the world a better place."

The words resonated with everyone. Arjuna and Karna, now understanding the value of camaraderie, shook hands. Their rivalry had turned into a bond of friendship.

As the sun set, the children, now friends, shared a meal together in the historic hotel. The journey to Hyderabad would continue, but they were no longer just individuals with powers. They were a team, bound by a shared purpose and an unbreakable bond.

"SOMETHING FEELS-OFF"

After their memorable experience at the Vedic Heritage Inn, Shiva, Krishna, Ram, Anju, Lakshman, and Saraswati resumed their journey to Hyderabad. The ride back was filled with laughter and the shared excitement of the recent events, yet a strange sense of unease lingered in the air.

Upon reaching Hyderabad, the group returned to their daily routines. They attended their classes at Rishi International School, trained in their respective sports, and spent time together, enjoying each other's company. However, something felt different. The familiarity of their surroundings seemed to have taken on an eerie quality, as if the world around them had subtly shifted.

Shiva noticed it first. During his meditation, he sensed a disturbance in the balance of energies. The usually serene and calm aura of the place was tinged with an unidentifiable tension. Krishna, with his keen intuition, felt a similar unease. The vibrant, bustling city seemed muted, and the people around them appeared distracted, as if they were moving through a haze.

Ram, ever vigilant, observed small changes in their environment. The normally lively streets seemed quieter, and the sky often took on a peculiar hue. Anju, with his boundless energy, found it difficult to stay focused, feeling an inexplicable restlessness. Lakshman, too, felt an underlying current of anxiety, though he couldn't pinpoint its source. Saraswati, in her wisdom, sensed that something significant had changed, though she couldn't discern what it was.

The group gathered at their usual spot, a serene park near their school, to discuss their feelings. "Have any of you noticed anything strange?" Shiva asked, breaking the silence.

Krishna nodded. "Yes, the city's energy feels off. It's like something is out of balance."

Ram added, "I've seen small changes too. The streets are quieter, and the people seem distracted."

Anju, usually the most animated, looked pensive. "I can't shake off this restlessness. It's like I'm missing something important."

Lakshman and Saraswati exchanged glances. "I've felt it too," Lakshman said. "There's an underlying tension, but I can't figure out why."

Saraswati spoke softly, "We need to investigate. Something has shifted, and we must understand what it is."

Determined to uncover the truth, the group decided to keep a close watch on their surroundings and look for any clues. They remained vigilant, paying attention to the smallest details, hoping to find the source of their unease.

Days turned into weeks, and the sense of discomfort grew. One evening, as they were walking home from school, they noticed a faint glow emanating from an old, abandoned temple on the outskirts of the city. Drawn by the strange light, they approached cautiously.

Inside the temple, they discovered an ancient relic pulsating with an otherworldly energy. As they examined it, the relic began to glow brighter, filling the room with a blinding light. When the light faded, they found themselves in a different realm, a place that felt both familiar and alien.

A figure emerged from the shadows, cloaked in mystery. "Welcome, chosen ones," the figure said, their voice echoing through the chamber. "You have sensed the disturbance. It is the work of Kaal, who has not been fully defeated. He has found a way to influence your world from the shadows."

Realization dawned upon them. The battle with Kaal was not truly over; he had managed to escape and was now subtly altering their reality. They needed to confront him once more, this time ensuring that his influence was completely eradicated.

With renewed determination, Shiva, Krishna, Ram, Anju, Lakshman, and Saraswati prepared for the ultimate confrontation. They knew they had to harness their divine powers and work together to restore balance and peace to their world.

As they stepped forward, ready to face Kaal again, they felt a surge of strength and unity. Together, they would overcome the darkness and ensure that their reality remained untainted, preserving the harmony they cherished so dearly.

"THE LIGHT OF UNITY"

As Shiva, Krishna, Ram, Anju, Lakshman, and Saraswati prepared to leave the ancient temple, ready to face Kaal once more, they heard familiar voices approaching. Turning towards the entrance, they saw Arjuna and Karna, who had also been drawn to the temple by the mysterious energy.

"Arjuna! Karna! What brings you here?" Krishna asked, his eyes reflecting both surprise and relief at their timely arrival.

Arjuna, still in his divine form, stepped forward. "We sensed the same disturbance you did. The energy in this place called out to us."

Karna nodded in agreement. "We couldn't ignore it. We knew something significant was happening here."

The group shared a brief but meaningful glance, understanding that their combined strength would be crucial in the battle to come. Together, they left the temple and stepped back into the world, now aware of the looming threat that Kaal posed.

Back in Hyderabad, the city's eerie quietness seemed even more pronounced. The team, now including Arjuna and Karna, gathered at their usual spot in the park to strategize.

Saraswati, her wisdom guiding them, spoke first. "Kaal is manipulating reality from the shadows. We need to find the source of his power and disrupt it."

Krishna added, "We must stay vigilant. His influence could be anywhere, subtly altering our world."

Ram, always the tactician, proposed, "We should split into smaller groups to cover more ground. Any signs of abnormal energy or behavior could lead us to Kaal."

The group agreed, and they divided into pairs: Shiva and Saraswati, Krishna and Arjuna, Ram and Karna, and Anju and Lakshman. Each pair set out in different directions, using their divine senses to detect any anomalies.

Shiva and Saraswati wandered through the bustling markets and serene temples, their senses heightened for any sign of Kaal's influence. In one quiet alley, they discovered a small talisman pulsing with dark energy. "This must be one of Kaal's tools," Shiva said, carefully taking the talisman.

Krishna and Arjuna moved through the busy streets, their keen eyes scanning for anything out of the ordinary. Near a busy intersection, they found a stone with intricate carvings that seemed to shimmer unnaturally. "We're on the right track," Arjuna remarked.

Ram and Karna explored the outskirts of the city, their combined strength making them a formidable team. In an abandoned warehouse, they stumbled upon a hidden chamber filled with ancient artifacts, all exuding a malevolent aura. "These must be amplifying Kaal's power," Karna observed.

Anju and Lakshman searched the parks and schools, their connection allowing them to work seamlessly together. In a deserted playground, they discovered a small, obsidian mirror that seemed to absorb light. "This has Kaal's essence all over it," Anju noted.

Regrouping at their meeting point, they shared their findings. Each item they had discovered was a conduit for Kaal's influence. By disrupting these conduits, they could weaken his hold on reality.

"We need to destroy these artifacts simultaneously," Saraswati advised. "Only then can we ensure Kaal's power is fully diminished."

With a plan in place, the group split up once more, each pair taking one of the artifacts. At the exact same moment, they channeled their divine energy into the items, shattering them and releasing bursts of pure light.

As the last artifact was destroyed, a tremor shook the ground. From the shadows, a figure emerged, cloaked in darkness—Kaal. His form was twisted and malevolent, a stark contrast to the divine light of the heroes.

"You may have weakened me, but I am far from defeated!" Kaal hissed, his voice echoing with malice.

The group united, their powers combining to form a radiant barrier of light. Shiva's trident, Krishna's flute, Ram's bow, Anju's mace, Lakshman's sword, Saraswati's veena, Arjuna's bow, and Karna's armor—all glowing with divine energy.

With a mighty battle cry, they launched their attack. Kaal fought back fiercely, but the unity and strength of the group were overwhelming. Their combined divine powers created a blinding explosion of light that engulfed Kaal, purging his darkness from the world.

When the light faded, Kaal was gone, his malevolent presence eradicated. The city of Hyderabad began to feel normal again, the eerie quietness replaced by the usual bustling energy.

Exhausted but victorious, the group returned to the park, their bond stronger than ever. "We did it," Krishna said, a smile spreading across his face.

Shiva nodded. "Together, we can overcome any darkness."

As they sat together, the sun setting behind them, they knew that their friendship and unity were their greatest strengths. No matter what challenges lay ahead, they would face them as one, ensuring that the light of their divine heritage would always shine brightly.

6

"The Uneasy Peace"

With Kaal defeated and his malevolent presence eradicated, the group of divine children returned to their daily lives in Hyderabad. The city slowly regained its normalcy, the eerie quietness replaced by the familiar sounds of bustling streets and lively chatter. Yet, an undercurrent of vigilance persisted among Shiva, Krishna, Ram, Anju, Lakshman, Saraswati, Arjuna, and Karna. They knew that even in times of peace, they must remain prepared for any threat that might arise.

At school, their friends and classmates noticed subtle changes in their demeanor. They appeared more focused, more thoughtful, and at times, slightly distant. Their teachers praised their increased concentration and participation, unaware of the extraordinary responsibilities they carried.

During breaks, the group often found themselves discussing their experiences in hushed tones, away from prying ears. They shared their dreams and fears, finding solace in each other's company. Despite their divine powers, they were still young, and the weight of their destiny sometimes felt overwhelming.

In the evenings, they gathered in the park near their school, a serene haven where they could relax and strategize without interruption. They often practiced their abilities in secret, honing their skills and exploring new aspects of their powers. These sessions were both training and bonding experiences, strengthening the trust and camaraderie among them.

The uneasy peace was a constant reminder that their battle with Kaal had been just one of many challenges they might face. They knew that threats could emerge from anywhere, and they vowed to stay vigilant, always ready to protect their world from any darkness that threatened it.

As the days passed, they also noticed subtle changes in their surroundings. The city seemed more vibrant, as if it was slowly recovering from an invisible burden. People smiled more, the air felt lighter, and there was a renewed sense of hope. The group took solace in knowing that their efforts had brought about this positive change, reaffirming their commitment to safeguarding their world.

Despite the underlying tension, they found moments of joy and normalcy in their daily lives. They laughed, played, and cherished the simple pleasures of being together. In these moments, they were not just warriors or divine beings; they were friends, united by a shared purpose and an unbreakable bond.

"School Days and Hidden Strengths"

At Rishi International School, the divine children seamlessly blended into their academic routines, their extraordinary abilities hidden beneath the guise of normalcy. Each day was a balancing act between their supernatural responsibilities and the mundane tasks of school life. Shiva and Saraswati's intellectual prowess was unparalleled, making them top performers in every subject. Their teachers admired their dedication, unaware of the divine wisdom that fueled their success.

Krishna and Arjuna dominated the sports field, their agility and coordination almost supernatural. They became the stars of the school's cricket team, leading their team to victory in every match. Ram, Anju, Lakshman, and Karna found their niches in various clubs and activities, bringing their unique strengths to everything they did. Ram's leadership shone in the debate club, Anju's energy was infectious in drama, Lakshman's strategic mind excelled in chess, and Karna's resilience made him a formidable athlete in track and field.

Despite their busy schedules, the group never missed their evening meetings in the park. These sessions were a blend of training, strategizing, and catching up on each other's lives. They shared their observations, discussed any subtle disturbances they noticed, and strengthened their bond, knowing that their unity was their greatest asset.

"The Whisper of Shadows"

One evening, as the sun dipped below the horizon, casting long shadows over the park, Shiva sensed a familiar disturbance. It was faint, almost imperceptible, but it stirred something deep within him. He shared his unease with the others, who quickly realized they had sensed it too.

"A whisper of shadows," Saraswati murmured, her eyes reflecting concern. "A disturbance in the balance."

Krishna's usually carefree demeanor turned serious. "We must investigate. If Kaal's influence has returned, we need to stop it before it grows."

Determined to uncover the source of the disturbance, they decided to keep a closer watch on their surroundings. They continued with their daily routines, but with heightened vigilance, ready to spring into action at the first sign of trouble.

The Hidden Library

Weeks passed, and the disturbances grew more frequent. Anomalies appeared throughout the city—lights flickering without cause, shadows moving independently, and eerie whispers in the wind. The group decided to seek answers in an ancient library rumored to hold secrets of the divine and the demonic.

The library, hidden in a secluded part of the city, was a vast repository of ancient knowledge. Its towering shelves were filled with scrolls and books, their pages containing the wisdom of ages. The group split up to search for any information on Kaal and his possible return.

Ram and Karna discovered a dusty tome detailing the history of Kaal, his rise to power, and his methods of manipulating reality. Anju and Lakshman found scrolls that described various artifacts of darkness and their functions. Saraswati, Shiva, Krishna, and Arjuna unearthed texts that spoke of rituals and spells that could summon or banish dark entities.

As they pieced together the information, a chilling realization dawned upon them. Kaal's influence had not been entirely eradicated; remnants of his power lingered, waiting to be reawakened.

Chapter 5: The Gathering Storm

With their newfound knowledge, the group knew they had to act quickly. They devised a plan to locate and neutralize any remaining artifacts of darkness before they could be used to restore Kaal's power. They split into pairs once again, each tasked with finding and destroying specific items.

Shiva and Saraswati ventured into the heart of the city, where they discovered a hidden shrine pulsing with dark energy. Using their combined divine powers, they shattered the shrine, dispelling its malevolent aura.

Krishna and Arjuna traveled to the outskirts, where they found a cave filled with dark artifacts. With precision and determination, they destroyed each item, nullifying its power.

Ram and Karna explored the rural areas, unearthing a buried chest containing cursed relics. They cleansed the items with divine light, ensuring they could no longer be used for evil.

Anju and Lakshman scoured the nearby forests, discovering an ancient altar dedicated to Kaal. With a mighty swing of Anju's mace and a decisive strike from Lakshman's sword, they dismantled the altar, breaking its connection to the dark forces.

Chapter 6: The Final Confrontation

Despite their efforts, the disturbances persisted. The group realized that there must be a central source of Kaal's lingering power, a core that needed to be destroyed to finally rid their world of his influence. Their search led them to an ancient temple hidden deep within a dense forest.

The temple, shrouded in darkness, radiated an ominous energy. As the group approached, they could feel the malevolent presence intensify. Inside, they found a dark altar, its surface covered in intricate runes and glowing with an eerie light.

Kaal's voice echoed through the temple. "You may have weakened me, but I am not defeated. My essence is eternal. You cannot destroy me."

With determination, the group prepared for the final battle. Shiva, Krishna, Ram, Anju, Lakshman, Saraswati, Arjuna, and Karna stood united, their divine powers combining to form a radiant shield of light.

Kaal materialized before them, his form a swirling mass of shadows and darkness. "This ends now," Shiva declared, his trident gleaming with divine energy.

The battle was fierce and relentless. Kaal's dark energy clashed with their divine light, creating a spectacle of power and strength. The temple trembled with the force of their conflict.

Chapter 7: The Power of Unity

Despite Kaal's formidable power, the group's unity and determination proved to be stronger. Each member contributed their unique abilities, creating a synergy that overwhelmed Kaal's darkness. Shiva's trident pierced through the shadows, Krishna's flute emitted a melody that disrupted the dark energy, Ram's arrows struck with divine precision, Anju's mace shattered the dark barriers, Lakshman's sword cut through the malevolent aura, Saraswati's veena filled the air with purifying vibrations, Arjuna's arrows found their mark, and Karna's armor shielded them from Kaal's attacks.

With a final surge of combined power, they unleashed a blinding explosion of light that enveloped Kaal, disintegrating his form and banishing his essence from their world.

Chapter 8: A New Dawn

As the light faded, the temple fell silent. The oppressive darkness that had once filled the air was replaced by a serene tranquility. The group stood together, their breaths heavy but their spirits lifted.

"We did it," Krishna said, his voice filled with relief and triumph.

Shiva nodded. "Kaal's influence is finally gone."

The group left the temple, the first rays of dawn breaking through the trees. The city of Hyderabad, now free from the lingering shadows, felt vibrant and alive once more.

Chapter 9: Reflections and Resolutions

Back in the city, the group gathered in the park to reflect on their journey. They had faced great challenges and emerged victorious, their bond stronger than ever.

Ram spoke first. "We've achieved something incredible. But we must remain vigilant. Our world will always have threats, and we must be ready to face them."

Saraswati added, "We have the strength and wisdom to protect our world. As long as we stand together, we can overcome any darkness."

Anju, with his characteristic enthusiasm, said, "And we'll keep training and getting stronger. We'll be ready for whatever comes next!"

Lakshman nodded. "Our unity is our greatest strength. As long as we remain united, nothing can defeat us."

Chapter 10: A Bright Future

As the days turned into weeks, life in Hyderabad returned to normal. The group continued their studies, sports, and activities, their divine powers now a well-kept secret. They remained vigilant, their senses attuned to any disturbances, but the city felt peaceful and safe.

Their experiences had taught them valuable lessons about friendship, unity, and the importance of using their gifts for the greater good. They knew that they would always be there for each other, ready to face any challenges that came their way.

In the quiet moments, they often reminisced about their adventures, the battles they had fought, and the bonds they had forged. They were not just friends; they were a family, united by destiny and strengthened by their shared purpose.

As the sun set over Hyderabad, casting a warm glow over the city, the group sat together in the park, enjoying the simple pleasures of life. They knew that their journey was far from over, but they were ready for whatever the future held.

With hearts full of hope and spirits unyielding, Shiva, Krishna, Ram, Anju, Lakshman, Saraswati, Arjuna, and Karna looked towards the horizon, confident in their ability to protect their world and preserve the light of their divine heritage.

The end of one journey marked the beginning of another, and they were prepared to face it together, united in purpose and bound by

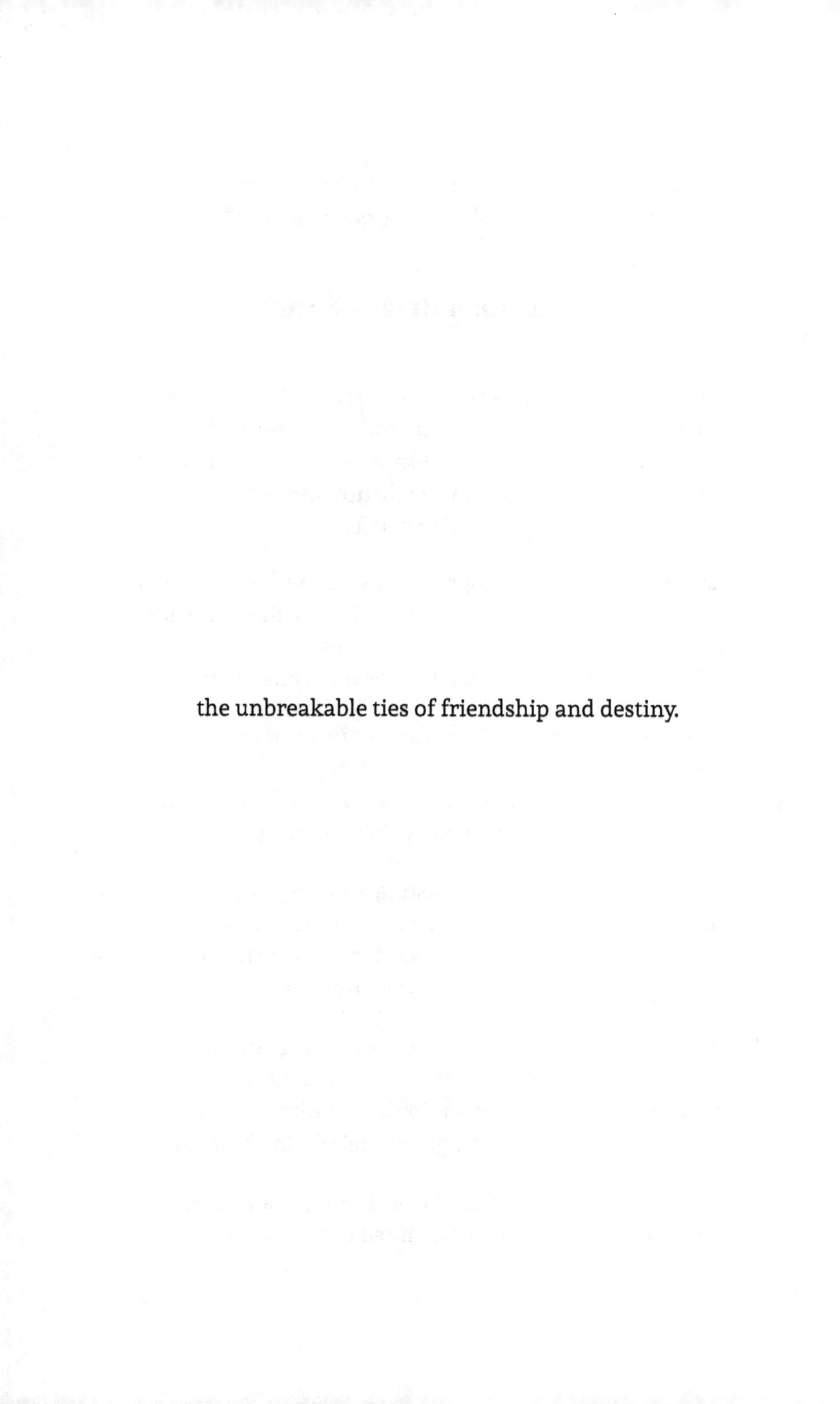

the unbreakable ties of friendship and destiny.

7
"CELEBRATIONS"

Diwali

The first major festival the group celebrated together after their victory over Kaal was Diwali, the Festival of Lights. Hyderabad was transformed into a city of sparkling lights and joyous sounds. Streets and homes were adorned with colorful rangoli, diyas, and strings of twinkling lights. The festive atmosphere was infectious, and the group was excited to participate in the celebrations.

Shiva and Saraswati led the preparations at Ram's house, where they all decided to gather. Saraswati's artistic skills were evident as she created intricate rangoli designs at the entrance, while Shiva set up rows of diyas, their warm glow illuminating the courtyard.

As evening fell, the group gathered to perform the Lakshmi Puja. They took turns reciting prayers and offering sweets to the goddess of wealth and prosperity. The air was filled with the scent of incense and the sound of devotional songs, creating a serene and sacred atmosphere.

After the puja, they moved outside to light fireworks. Krishna and Arjuna, ever the competitive spirits, tried to outdo each other with their fireworks displays. Anju and Lakshman cheered them on, laughing and clapping at each burst of color in the sky. Ram and Karna, usually serious and composed, joined in the fun with surprising enthusiasm, their faces lit up with childlike delight.

Saraswati captured these moments on her phone, ensuring that the memories of their first Diwali together were preserved. They spent the night sharing stories, eating delicious sweets, and enjoying the company of friends who had become family.

The Joy of Holi

As winter gave way to spring, the festival of Holi approached. Known as the festival of colors, Holi was a time of joy, playfulness, and vibrant celebrations. The group decided to celebrate it in a large open field near their school, where they could indulge in the festivities without any restrictions.

On the morning of Holi, they gathered early, dressed in old clothes, ready to be drenched in colors. Shiva and Saraswati brought bags of organic gulal, while Krishna and Arjuna filled water balloons and water guns with colored water. Ram and Karna prepared packets of dry colors, while Anju and Lakshman set up a music system to play festive songs.

The celebrations began with a burst of color as Krishna mischievously threw a handful of gulal at Arjuna, who retaliated immediately. Soon, everyone was engaged in a joyful riot of colors. They chased each other, laughing and shouting, their faces and clothes covered in every shade imaginable.

Saraswati, usually composed and serene, joined in with enthusiasm, her white dress quickly turning into a canvas of colors. Ram and Karna, always competitive, challenged each other to see who could stay the cleanest the longest, a challenge they both quickly lost as Anju and Lakshman ambushed them with water balloons.

After hours of play, they sat down to enjoy a feast of traditional Holi delicacies. They shared gujiyas, thandai, and other sweets, their laughter echoing across the field. As the day ended, they were tired but happy, their spirits uplifted by the joyous celebrations.

Ganesh Chaturthi Festivities

The next big celebration was Ganesh Chaturthi, the festival dedicated to Lord Ganesha. The group decided to install a Ganesha idol in Krishna's home, where they could perform the rituals together. They spent days preparing for the festival, decorating the house with flowers, lights, and intricate mandalas.

On the day of Ganesh Chaturthi, they welcomed the beautifully adorned idol of Lord Ganesha with chants of "Ganapati Bappa Morya!" Shiva and Saraswati led the rituals, guiding the group through the various prayers and offerings. The house was filled with the scent of fresh flowers, incense, and the rhythmic sound of drums and bells.

The group participated enthusiastically in the daily aarti, singing bhajans and clapping in unison. Krishna's musical talents shone as he played the flute, adding a melodious touch to the celebrations. Anju and Lakshman, known for their energy, danced joyfully, their movements reflecting their devotion and happiness.

During the ten days of the festival, the group organized cultural programs, inviting friends and neighbors to join in the celebrations. They performed plays depicting stories of Lord Ganesha, sang devotional songs, and shared the delicious prasad with everyone.

On the final day, they carried the idol in a grand procession to the nearby lake for the immersion ceremony. Amidst chants and music, they bid farewell to Lord Ganesha, praying for his return next year. The immersion was a bittersweet moment, filled with emotions and memories of the joyous days spent together.

Navratri and Dussehra

As autumn approached, the city prepared for Navratri and Dussehra, festivals that celebrated the victory of good over evil. The group decided to celebrate these festivals with great fervor, participating in the traditional Garba and Dandiya Raas dances.

They visited the beautifully decorated pandals, where large idols of Goddess Durga were installed. Each night, they joined the community in dancing around the idol, their colorful attire swirling in rhythm with the beats of the drums and the melodies of the songs. Saraswati, with her grace and elegance, led the group, teaching them the intricate steps of the Garba and Dandiya.

Krishna and Arjuna, known for their agility, quickly mastered the dance moves, adding their flair to the traditional steps. Anju and Lakshman, always full of energy, kept the group's spirits high, encouraging everyone to dance with enthusiasm. Ram and Karna, though initially hesitant, soon joined in, their serious demeanor giving way to joyous laughter.

On the tenth day, they celebrated Dussehra, witnessing the dramatic reenactment of Lord Ram's victory over Ravana. They watched in awe as the effigies of Ravana, Meghnath, and Kumbhkaran were set ablaze, symbolizing the triumph of good over evil. The sky lit up with fireworks, and the air was filled with cheers and applause.

The group felt a deep connection to the story of Dussehra, having faced and defeated their own version of Ravana in the form of Kaal. They renewed their commitment to stand against evil and protect their world, drawing inspiration from the festival's message.

The Serenity of Raksha Bandhan

Raksha Bandhan was a special festival for the group, symbolizing the bond of protection and love between brothers and sisters. They gathered at Saraswati's house, where she and Anju had prepared rakhis for each of the boys.

The ceremony began with Saraswati tying rakhis on the wrists of Shiva, Krishna, Ram, Lakshman, Arjuna, and Karna. Each boy promised to protect her and be there for her in times of need. Anju followed, tying rakhis and sharing her love and laughter with each of them.

In return, the boys gave their sisters gifts, tokens of their appreciation and love. They shared sweets, exchanged heartfelt messages, and reminisced about their adventures and the bond that united them.

The simplicity and purity of Raksha Bandhan touched everyone deeply. It was a reminder of the strength they drew from each other, not just in battle but in everyday life. The festival reinforced their commitment to protect and support one another, strengthening their bond as a family.

The Grandeur of Durga Puja

Durga Puja was a festival of grand celebrations, and the group decided to experience it in its full glory by visiting the famous pandals in the city. The elaborate decorations, the vibrant colors, and the rhythmic beats of the dhak drums created an electrifying atmosphere.

They visited different pandals, admiring the beautiful idols of Goddess Durga, each depicting her in various forms and postures. Saraswati explained the significance of the festival, narrating stories of Durga's battles against the demons and her ultimate victory.

In the evenings, they participated in the aarti and bhog distribution. They sang and danced in the traditional style, joining the community in the joyous celebrations. Krishna and Arjuna's enthusiasm was infectious, drawing even the shyest members of the group into the festivities.

On the final day, they witnessed the grand immersion procession, where the idols were carried to the river amidst music and dance. They joined the crowd in bidding farewell to the goddess, praying for her return next year.

Christmas

Christmas brought a different kind of joy to the group. Although not a traditional festival for most of them, they embraced the spirit of the season with enthusiasm. They decided to celebrate it at Karna's house, decorating a Christmas tree and hanging stockings.

Saraswati and Anju baked cookies and cakes, filling the house with the delightful aroma of freshly baked goods. Shiva and Krishna strung lights and ornaments on the tree, while Ram and Lakshman set up a nativity scene.

On Christmas Eve, they exchanged gifts, each one carefully chosen to reflect their bond and understanding of each other. They sang carols, with Krishna playing the flute and Saraswati accompanying him on the veena. Anju and Lakshman performed a playful skit, bringing laughter and cheer to the gathering.

The highlight of the evening was the arrival of Santa Claus, played by Arjuna, who distributed gifts and chocolates to everyone. The group's laughter and joy echoed through the house, creating memories that would last a lifetime.

8

"The Tiger Among Us"

The sun was setting, casting a warm golden hue over the sprawling campus of Rishi International School. The group of friends – Shiva, Krishna, Ram, Anju, Lakshman, Saraswati, Arjuna, and Karna – were gathered under their favorite tree, recounting their latest adventures and sharing laughs.

Meanwhile, a new face had quietly made his way into the school. Abhi, the new student, was an enigma to everyone. He moved through the hallways with a calm and composed demeanor, his eyes often hidden behind a curtain of dark hair. His physique was lean but strong, with an air of quiet confidence that intrigued those who noticed him.

Abhi spent most of his time in the library, immersed in books on various subjects. He had a particular fondness for history and mythology, often found poring over ancient texts and scriptures. His behavior was so calm and focused that many students mistook him for an introvert, someone who preferred solitude over social interaction.

During lunch breaks, while other students chatted and played, Abhi could be seen sitting alone under a tree, eating his meals in silence. He observed his surroundings with keen interest, his sharp eyes missing nothing. Despite his solitary nature, there was an aura of strength and determination about him that hinted at something more than met the eye.

One day, as the group of friends were deep in conversation, they noticed Abhi sitting on a nearby bench, absorbed in a thick book. Krishna, always curious and friendly, decided to approach him. "Hey, you're Abhi, right? New to the school?" he asked, flashing his trademark smile.

Abhi looked up, momentarily surprised, but then nodded with a small smile of his own. "Yes, I joined last week."

Krishna introduced him to the rest of the group. They welcomed him warmly, but it was clear that Abhi was still guarded, his eyes always alert and cautious. Despite this, they included him in their conversations, slowly breaking down the walls he had built around himself.

Days turned into weeks, and Abhi started to feel more at ease with the group. He admired their camaraderie and the way they stood by each other, reminding him of the values he held dear. One evening, as they were all gathered after school, sharing stories and snacks, Abhi decided it was time to reveal his secret.

He took a deep breath and looked at his new friends, their faces expectant and kind. "There's something I need to tell you all," he began, his voice steady but filled with a hint of vulnerability. "I haven't been completely honest about who I am."

The group fell silent, their curiosity piqued. Abhi stood up, his posture suddenly shifting. His calm demeanor gave way to a more assertive stance, his movements becoming fluid and graceful. "I have a unique ability," he continued. "I can transform my physique and fighting style to resemble that of a tiger."

With that, he demonstrated a few swift, powerful moves, his body moving with the precision and agility of the majestic animal. The group watched in awe, recognizing the same divine essence they possessed within him.

Abhi looked at them, his eyes filled with a mix of hope and uncertainty. "I've always kept this part of me hidden, afraid of how people might react. But seeing how you all embrace your abilities and each other, I felt it was time to share mine."

Shiva stepped forward, placing a reassuring hand on Abhi's shoulder. "Welcome to the team, Abhi. You're one of us now."

As they stood together, under the fading light of the day, a new bond was formed. With Abhi joining their ranks, the group felt even stronger, ready to face whatever challenges lay ahead, united by their shared secrets and the promise of friendship.

ABHI

9

"Back to School & the Distribution of Chocolates"

It was Arjuna's birthday, and the air was filled with excitement as he went around the school, distributing chocolates to his friends and classmates. The bell had just rung for Mr. Mukherji's English class, and the students were settling into their seats, eagerly anticipating the lesson.

Mr. Mukherji, known for his wit and humor, walked into the classroom with a mischievous grin on his face. He was a tall man with a bushy mustache and expressive eyes that twinkled with amusement.

"Good afternoon, class!" he boomed, his voice echoing through the room.

"Good afternoon, Sir!" the students chorused back, their voices tinged with anticipation.

"Today is a special day," Mr. Mukherji began, "because we have a birthday boy among us. Arjuna, please come forward."

Arjuna, slightly embarrassed but smiling, stood up and walked to the front of the class, holding a large box of chocolates.

Mr. Mukherji clasped his hands together dramatically. "Ah, birthdays! A time of joy, a time of celebration, and most importantly, a time of chocolates!" He winked at the class, causing a ripple of laughter.

"Now, Arjuna," Mr. Mukherji continued, "before you distribute these delightful treats, I have a small request. Since today is your day, why don't you grace us with a recitation of your favorite poem?"

Arjuna, who loved literature almost as much as he loved archery, nodded enthusiastically. He began reciting a stanza from one of his favorite poems, his voice clear and confident.

As Arjuna recited, Mr. Mukherji moved to his desk and picked up a ruler. He then proceeded to mime conducting an orchestra, using the ruler as a baton, waving it dramatically in the air in sync with Arjuna's recital. The class burst into giggles, trying to suppress their laughter so as not to interrupt Arjuna.

When Arjuna finished, the classroom erupted in applause. Mr. Mukherji bowed deeply, as if he were the one being applauded, then straightened up with a flourish.

"Bravo, Arjuna! A performance worthy of the finest stages!" he exclaimed. "Now, on to the most important part of any birthday – the chocolates!"

Arjuna began to distribute the chocolates, and Mr. Mukherji's antics continued. He tiptoed behind Arjuna, mimicking his every move, exaggerating the way he handed out the chocolates. The class was in stitches, trying to keep their laughter in check as Arjuna made his way around the room.

When Arjuna reached Mr. Mukherji, the teacher took a chocolate with a grandiose gesture and said, "Ah, thank you, dear Arjuna. You know, I once read that chocolates are the food of the gods. And if that's true, then today, we are all little gods, thanks to you!"

The class roared with laughter, and Arjuna, now fully enjoying the moment, joined in.

Mr. Mukherji held up his chocolate and declared, "To Arjuna, our birthday boy! May your aim always be true, whether it's with a bow or in life. And may your chocolates always be plentiful!"

The students cheered and clapped, raising their chocolates in a toast. Arjuna, beaming from ear to ear, felt the warmth of his classmates' affection and the humor that Mr. Mukherji had brought to his special day.

As the laughter died down and the class began to settle, Mr. Mukherji wiped a tear of mirth from his eye and said, "Alright, enough fun for now. Let's get back to the wonders of English literature. But remember, life is always sweeter with a bit of laughter and, of course, chocolates!"

The students nodded, still grinning, and the lesson continued with an air of happiness and camaraderie that only a great teacher like Mr. Mukherji could inspire.

"THE CHEMISTRY OF LAUGHTER"

The chemistry lab was meticulously organized, every beaker, test tube, and flask in its proper place. Mr. Kalyan, the chemistry teacher, was known for his strict demeanor and no-nonsense attitude. His deep, authoritative voice commanded respect, and his lessons were always conducted with precision and discipline.

Arjuna, still basking in the afterglow of his birthday celebrations, had the task of distributing chocolates to all the teachers. With a bit of trepidation, he approached the chemistry lab, clutching a box of chocolates. The thought of facing Mr. Kalyan, who was known for his rigorous approach, made him nervous.

He hesitated at the door, took a deep breath, and knocked softly.

"Enter," came Mr. Kalyan's stern voice from within.

Arjuna slowly opened the door and stepped inside, the box of chocolates clutched tightly in his hands. The students in the lab looked up, their curiosity piqued by Arjuna's unusual visit. Mr. Kalyan, wearing his lab coat and safety goggles, was engrossed in preparing some chemical mixtures at his desk.

"Good afternoon, Sir," Arjuna began, his voice a bit shaky.

Mr. Kalyan looked up, his expression softening slightly. "Ah, Arjuna. What brings you here?"

"I... I came to distribute chocolates," Arjuna said, holding out the box. "It's my birthday today."

Mr. Kalyan raised an eyebrow, a rare smile playing at the corners of his mouth. "Is that so? Well, I must say, this is quite an unexpected pleasure."

Arjuna, unsure how to respond, fumbled with the box. "I... um, I hope you like them, Sir."

Mr. Kalyan took a chocolate with a nod, his gaze shifting from the candy to Arjuna's apprehensive face. "You know, Arjuna, I rarely get to enjoy such sweet moments in my chemistry class," he said, his tone lighter than usual.

Arjuna's eyes widened slightly, surprised by Mr. Kalyan's attempt at humor. "Really, Sir?"

"Yes," Mr. Kalyan continued, with a twinkle in his eye, "the closest I come to sweets is when I mix sugar with sulfuric acid. But as you might imagine, that doesn't end well for the sugar!"

The students in the lab chuckled, and Arjuna's nervousness began to ease. Mr. Kalyan's rare display of humor made the atmosphere in the room feel more relaxed.

"Thank you, Arjuna," Mr. Kalyan said, his voice taking on a gentler tone. "It's nice to see that chemistry isn't the only thing that can bring a smile to our faces."

Arjuna smiled, feeling a bit more at ease. "You're welcome, Sir. I hope you have a great day."

Mr. Kalyan gave a rare, genuine smile as he accepted the chocolate. "I'm sure I will, thanks to you. And remember, just like in chemistry, it's the little things that sometimes make the biggest difference."

As Arjuna turned to leave, he couldn't help but feel a sense of relief. Mr. Kalyan's unexpected joke and kind words had lightened the mood, making the encounter much more pleasant than he had anticipated.

As the door closed behind Arjuna, Mr. Kalyan looked down at the chocolate in his hand, a thoughtful expression on his face. The students, observing their normally stern teacher in this rare, relaxed moment, felt a newfound respect for him.

"Well," Mr. Kalyan said, turning back to his class with a slight grin, "let's get back to the chemistry of reactions. But remember, even in the strictest of labs, there's always room for a bit of sweetness."

The class laughed, their spirits lifted by the unexpected moment of levity. The lab buzzed with a renewed energy, and Mr. Kalyan, though still strict, was seen in a new, more relatable light.

"ARJUNA'S BIRTHDAY PARTY"

The evening sun cast a warm, golden glow over Arjuna's house, setting the stage for his birthday celebration. The backyard was decorated with colorful streamers and balloons, and a large table was set up with an assortment of snacks and treats. Laughter and cheerful chatter filled the air as Arjuna's friends arrived, eager to join in the festivities.

Arjuna, dressed in a casual yet stylish outfit, was busy greeting his friends and making sure everything was perfect. His excitement was palpable as he showed everyone around and introduced them to his family.

The guests, including Shiva, Krishna, Ram, Anju, Lakshman, and Saraswati, gathered around the table, enjoying the delicious food and exchanging stories. The atmosphere was lively, with games and music adding to the celebratory mood.

As the sun began to set, Arjuna's mother, Mrs. Sharma, stepped out into the backyard with a bright smile. She was holding a large, beautifully decorated birthday cake with candles flickering on top. She was a warm and affectionate woman with a kind face and a motherly presence.

"Arjuna, dear, come here!" she called out, her voice carrying across the yard.

Arjuna turned, his face lighting up as he saw his mother approaching with the cake. "Mom! The cake looks amazing!"

His friends gathered around, eagerly anticipating the cake-cutting ceremony. Mrs. Sharma placed the cake on the table and looked at Arjuna with a loving smile. "Happy Birthday, Ajju!" she said warmly.

Arjuna's face turned bright red at the use of his childhood nickname. The name "Ajju" was something only his family used, and hearing it in front of his friends made him feel both embarrassed and amused.

The friends, noticing Arjuna's reaction, couldn't help but burst into laughter. Krishna, with a grin, nudged Arjuna playfully. "Ajju, huh? I didn't know you had such a cute nickname!"

Shiva and Ram exchanged knowing glances, their laughter joining in. "Looks like someone's blush is getting the spotlight today!" Ram teased, adding to the playful banter.

Arjuna tried to hide his blush behind his hands, but the laughter from his friends and the affectionate teasing from his mother only made him blush more deeply. "Mom, can't you just call me Arjuna?" he said, half laughing and half embarrassed.

Mrs. Sharma laughed softly, her eyes twinkling with affection. "Oh, come on, Ajju. It's your special day. Let me enjoy calling you that just once more!"

The laughter continued as Arjuna's friends gathered around the cake, ready to sing the birthday song. As they sang, Arjuna couldn't help but smile, the warmth of the moment melting away any lingering embarrassment.

When the song ended and Arjuna blew out the candles, his friends cheered and clapped, their spirits high with the joy of the celebration. The rest of the evening was filled with games, dancing, and more laughter. The playful nickname had become a fond memory of the day, adding a personal touch to the joyous occasion.

As the party continued, Arjuna felt a sense of contentment, surrounded by friends and family who made his birthday truly special. The nickname "Ajju" would always be a reminder of the love and warmth he received from those closest to him, making his birthday an unforgettable celebration.

The Unexpected Performance

As the birthday party continued, the laughter and chatter created a lively buzz in the backyard. The guests enjoyed the festivities, with music playing softly in the background. The sun had set, and the twinkling fairy lights added a magical ambiance to the evening.

Arjuna's friends were engaged in a game of charades when Abhi, who had been relatively quiet throughout the party, stepped up to the center of the backyard. He had been sitting on the sidelines, observing the merriment with his usual calm demeanor.

"Hey, everyone!" Abhi called out, capturing everyone's attention. The guests turned to look at him, curiosity piqued by his sudden decision to take center stage.

Arjuna's eyes widened in surprise. "Abhi? What's up?"

Abhi, with a serene expression, smiled slightly. "I'd like to perform a song for Arjuna. I hope you all don't mind."

A murmur of excitement rippled through the crowd. Arjuna looked at Abhi with curiosity and admiration. "Sure, Abhi! I'd love to hear it."

Abhi walked over to the makeshift stage area where the party's sound system was set up. He picked up a microphone and took a deep breath, his calm demeanor contrasting with the lively atmosphere. The guests, intrigued by this unexpected turn, gathered around, eager to see what Abhi had prepared.

With a gentle nod, Abhi began to sing. His voice was soft yet powerful, filling the air with a soothing melody. The song he chose was a beautiful, heartfelt piece about friendship and the journey of life. It was a song that spoke of resilience, hope, and the joy of shared moments.

As Abhi sang, the guests fell silent, captivated by the emotional depth of his performance. His voice flowed effortlessly, carrying the melody with grace and sincerity. The lyrics resonated deeply, touching the hearts of everyone present.

Arjuna, who had been caught off guard, watched in awe. Abhi's performance was unexpected but incredibly moving. The earlier laughter and playful banter seemed to fade into the background, replaced by the poignant beauty of the song.

Mrs. Sharma, standing nearby, watched with a proud smile. She had always known her son's friends were special, but Abhi's unexpected talent added a new dimension to the evening.

When Abhi reached the final notes of the song, there was a moment of hushed silence. The guests were so absorbed in the performance that they almost forgot to clap. As the last note lingered in the air, the crowd erupted into applause, their cheers echoing in the cool evening air.

Abhi smiled modestly, his calm demeanor returning as he set the microphone down. He looked over at Arjuna, who was visibly moved. "I hope you enjoyed it," Abhi said softly.

Arjuna, still glowing from the performance, approached Abhi with a heartfelt expression. "That was amazing, Abhi. Thank you so much. It really made my birthday even more special."

The friends gathered around Abhi, congratulating him and expressing their appreciation for his beautiful performance. Krishna gave him a friendly nudge. "I didn't know you had such a hidden talent, Abhi! That was incredible.”

Shiva and Ram joined in the praise, their admiration clear. “You should definitely perform more often!” Shiva exclaimed.

Abhi, though modest, seemed pleased by the positive response. “I’m glad you all enjoyed it.”

As the evening continued, the mood of the party was uplifted by Abhi’s unexpected performance. The guests chatted excitedly about the beautiful song, and the birthday celebration carried on with renewed energy. Abhi’s performance had added a special touch to the event, making it a night to remember for everyone, especially Arjuna.

THE ULTIMATE MOVIE NIGHT

As the evening deepened and the stars began to twinkle in the clear night sky, the mood of the party shifted to a more relaxed and cozy atmosphere. The backyard, which had been bustling with energy, was now transformed into a perfect setting for movie night.

Mrs. Sharma had set up a large outdoor screen and arranged comfy seating with bean bags, cushions, and blankets spread out across the lawn. String lights and lanterns created a warm, inviting glow, making the space feel like an outdoor theater.

movie night set up

"Alright, everyone!" Mrs. Sharma announced, clapping her hands to gather attention. "It's time for the movie night! I hope you're all ready to enjoy a great film under the stars."

The guests cheered and eagerly took their seats. The excitement was palpable as they settled in, making themselves comfortable. Arjuna, with his friends around him, looked thrilled. The birthday party had been fantastic so far, and the promise of a movie night was the perfect way to end the evening.

Abhi, who had been more reserved during the party, now seemed visibly relaxed, joining the others on a large bean bag. Krishna, always the enthusiastic one, was chatting animatedly about the movie selection. "I heard we're watching a classic adventure film tonight. This is going to be awesome!"

Shiva, Ram, Anju, and Saraswati gathered around, exchanging their favorite movie snacks and making themselves comfortable. The table near the screen was laden with popcorn, nachos, candy, and soda. The aroma of buttery popcorn filled the air, adding to the excitement.

As the lights dimmed and the movie began, the large screen flickered to life. The familiar opening scene of the film appeared, and the crowd let out a collective cheer. Everyone settled in, the sounds of rustling blankets and popcorn crunching fading into the background.

The movie was a classic adventure film that had something for everyone—action, humor, and heartwarming moments. Laughter erupted from the audience at the film's funny scenes, and gasps of excitement filled the air during the thrilling moments.

During one particularly tense scene, Arjuna looked over at Abhi, who was completely engrossed in the movie. Arjuna couldn't help but smile at how Abhi had seamlessly blended into the group, enjoying the movie as much as anyone else.

As the film progressed, Mrs. Sharma occasionally popped in with trays of snacks, making sure everyone had enough to munch on. Her thoughtful gestures were met with appreciative smiles and nods from the guests.

The climax of the movie brought a collective gasp and then a round of applause as the heroes triumphed. The friends cheered and clapped, their enjoyment evident. Even Mr. Kalyan, who had joined the party after his evening classes, was seen laughing and clapping along with the rest of the group.

When the credits began to roll, the guests reluctantly left their cozy spots to gather around the refreshment table. The conversation was lively as everyone shared their favorite moments from the film.

"That was incredible!" Krishna exclaimed. "I didn't expect such a thrilling ending!"

Saraswati agreed, "The movie had everything—action, humor, and a great storyline. It was the perfect choice!"

Abhi, still in his quiet and composed manner, added, "It was a great experience. Sometimes, it's nice to unwind with a good film and good company."

As the night wound down, the group lingered, reluctant to end the party. The movie had been the perfect finale to Arjuna's birthday celebration, adding a touch of magic to an already wonderful evening.

The friends and family chatted about the film and shared their plans for future gatherings. The atmosphere was filled with contentment and joy, a testament to the success of Arjuna's birthday party. As the last guests began to leave, Arjuna felt a deep sense of satisfaction, knowing that this was a night he would always cherish.

"THE MYSTERIOUS ENCOUNTER"

The night was winding down after a successful movie party. The backyard, now quiet, was strewn with the remnants of the evening's festivities—discarded popcorn bags, empty soda cans, and cozy blankets. Arjuna and his friends had all settled into their makeshift sleeping arrangements, drifting off to sleep under the canopy of stars.

Around two hours into the night, an eerie calm settled over the backyard. The gentle sounds of crickets and the rustling of leaves were the only noises, but the peaceful atmosphere was abruptly disturbed. One by one, the friends began to stir from their slumber, their dreams interrupted by a strange and unsettling sensation.

Arjuna, half-awake, could sense something off. He opened his eyes but saw nothing but darkness. His heart raced as he tried to focus on the figure he thought he saw—a black, shadowy presence that seemed to loom in the dim light of the moon.

Krishna, who had been dreaming of an epic quest, awoke with a start. He rubbed his eyes and squinted into the darkness, trying to make sense of the vague, indistinct shape that had flickered before him.

Shiva, Anju, and the others slowly woke up, their faces showing confusion and concern. "Did anyone else see that?" Anju asked, her voice trembling slightly.

"I thought I saw something too," Ram admitted. "But it was gone before I could really see what it was."

Saraswati, who had been deep in sleep, felt a shiver down her spine. "It felt... strange. Like a presence that wasn't supposed to be here."

The strange sensation lingered for a few moments before fading away, leaving the friends feeling unsettled. Despite their attempts to reassure each other, sleep eluded them for the rest of the night, their minds racing with questions and fears.

The next morning, the group gathered at school, still feeling the effects of their disturbed night. They exchanged stories and tried to piece together what had happened.

Arjuna, still processing the eerie encounter, was relieved to see that his friends had also experienced the strange presence. "So, did anyone figure out what that was?" he asked, trying to sound casual but clearly worried.

Krishna, scratching his head, said, "I've been thinking about it all night. It felt like something from a myth or legend."

At that moment, Abhi, who had been quietly listening, spoke up. His eyes were bright with interest. "You know, it sounds like something out of a mythological story. It might have been Narkasur."

Arjuna and his friends looked at Abhi, intrigued. "Narkasur?" Arjuna repeated. "Who's that?"

Abhi nodded enthusiastically. "Yes, Narkasur. In mythological tales, he was a powerful demon king. He's often depicted as a dark, shadowy figure who brings fear and chaos. His presence is known to unsettle those who encounter him, and his stories are associated with strange, ominous feelings."

Saraswati, who had a keen interest in mythology, added, "I've heard of him. According to the stories, Narkasur's spirit is said to roam in search of those who disturb the balance of the world."

Krishna, now fully engaged, said, "That would make sense. The feeling we had was definitely unsettling and not of this world."

The friends gathered around Abhi, eager to hear more. He continued, "Narkasur's legend has various interpretations, but the common thread is his presence being tied to disruptions and fear. It's fascinating, isn't it?"

The group nodded, their initial fear giving way to a sense of curiosity and excitement. The idea of having encountered a mythological figure added a layer of intrigue to their experience.

As the school day continued, the friends couldn't stop discussing the mysterious encounter and Abhi's insights. They began to speculate about what the encounter could mean and whether there was a deeper significance to their experience.

Arjuna, though still a bit unsettled, felt a sense of wonder. "It's amazing how mythology and real life can sometimes intersect. Even if it was just a dream, it's something we'll remember."

The group agreed, their conversation animated as they delved into mythological stories and legends. The mysterious figure of the night had turned into a shared adventure, sparking their imaginations and strengthening their bond.

As the day went on, the friends felt a renewed sense of camaraderie, their experience drawing them closer together. The eerie encounter had left them with more questions than answers, but it had also opened up a new chapter of exploration and wonder in their lives.

10

The Geometry of Triangles

The bell rang, signaling the start of their math class. The students of 9th grade, including Shiva, Krishna, Ram, Anji, Lakshman, Saraswati, Arjun, Karna, and Abhi, settled into their seats, ready for the lesson. Mr. Bhattacharya, their enthusiastic and slightly eccentric math teacher, walked in with a broad smile and a stack of papers.

"Good morning, class!" Mr. Bhattacharya greeted them, his voice full of energy. "Today, we are going to explore the fascinating world of triangles. Triangles are the building blocks of geometry, and they hold many secrets. Let's dive in!"

He turned to the whiteboard and began drawing a series of triangles. "First, let's review the basics. A triangle has three sides, three angles, and the sum of its interior angles is always 180 degrees. Can anyone tell me the different types of triangles based on their angles?"

Krishna raised his hand, eager to answer. "There are three types: acute, where all angles are less than 90 degrees; right, where one angle is exactly 90 degrees; and obtuse, where one angle is greater than 90 degrees."

"Excellent, Krishna!" Mr. Bhattacharya said, nodding in approval. "Now, what about the types of triangles based on their sides?"

Saraswati chimed in, "Equilateral, where all three sides are equal; isosceles, where two sides are equal; and scalene, where all sides are different lengths."

"Correct, Saraswati!" Mr. Bhattacharya continued, "Today, we'll delve deeper into these concepts and learn about some important theorems related to triangles. Let's start with the Pythagorean Theorem. Who can state the theorem for me?"

Arjun stood up confidently, "In a right triangle, the square of the hypotenuse is equal to the sum of the squares of the other two sides."

"Well said, Arjun! Let's see this in action," Mr. Bhattacharya drew a right triangle on the board and labeled the sides. "If this side is 'a,' this side is 'b,' and the hypotenuse is 'c,' then according to the Pythagorean Theorem, we have $a^2 + b^2 = c^2$. Let's try an example. If 'a' is 3 and 'b' is 4, what is 'c'?"

Anji quickly calculated, "Using the theorem, $3^2 + 4^2 = 9 + 16 = 25$, so $c^2 = 25$. Therefore, 'c' is 5."

"Perfect, Anji! Now let's move on to another interesting concept: the properties of the angles in a triangle." Mr. Bhattacharya sketched an isosceles triangle. "In an isosceles triangle, the angles opposite the equal sides are also equal. Can anyone explain why this is the case?"

Ram raised his hand, "It's because if two sides are equal, then the two base angles must also be equal to maintain the balance of the triangle's structure."

"Exactly, Ram! Let's prove this using congruent triangles." Mr. Bhattacharya drew a perpendicular bisector from the vertex angle to the base of the isosceles triangle, creating two congruent right triangles. "As you can see, these two triangles are congruent by the hypotenuse-leg theorem, which means the base angles are equal."

The students followed along, their interest piqued by the geometric proofs. Mr. Bhattacharya continued, "Now, let's talk about the triangle inequality theorem. This theorem states that the sum of the lengths of any two sides of a triangle must be greater than the length of the third side. Why do you think this is important?"

Abhi, who had been quietly absorbing the lesson, spoke up, "It ensures that the three sides can actually form a triangle. If the sum of two sides were equal to or less than the third side, it wouldn't be possible to close the shape into a triangle."

"Very insightful, Abhi!" Mr. Bhattacharya exclaimed. "Understanding these fundamental properties is crucial for solving more complex problems in geometry."

He then handed out a worksheet with various triangle problems, ranging from calculating side lengths using the Pythagorean Theorem to proving angle properties and applying the triangle inequality theorem. "Work on these problems in pairs. Discuss your solutions and help each other out. Remember, geometry is all about visualization and logical reasoning."

Shiva paired up with Krishna, Ram with Anji, Lakshman with Saraswati, and Arjun with Karna. Abhi, the newest member of the group, joined a nearby pair to observe and learn.

As they worked through the problems, the classroom buzzed with discussion and collaborative problem-solving. Shiva and Krishna debated the best approach to a challenging proof, while Ram and Anji quickly calculated side lengths using the Pythagorean Theorem. Lakshman and Saraswati methodically worked through angle properties, and Arjun and Karna found themselves in a friendly competition to see who could solve the problems faster.

Abhi, although initially reserved, started to contribute more as he became comfortable with the group. His sharp analytical mind and unique perspective added value to the discussions, earning him the respect and camaraderie of his classmates.

Mr. Bhattacharya walked around the room, offering guidance and encouragement. He was pleased to see the students so engaged and enthusiastic about the topic.

As the class drew to a close, Mr. Bhattacharya addressed the students, "Great work today, everyone! Triangles may seem simple, but they hold the key to understanding much of geometry. Keep practicing, and you'll uncover even more fascinating properties and theorems."

The bell rang, and the students gathered their materials, energized by the lesson. As they left the classroom, they chatted excitedly about the next class, their minds buzzing with geometric concepts and new insights.

Discovering Cultural Roots

The bell rang for the next period, and the students of 9th grade made their way to their Telugu class. Mr. Rajasekhar, their Telugu teacher, was known for his deep knowledge of the language and its rich cultural heritage. The classroom was decorated with posters of famous Telugu poets and writers, and there was a quiet reverence among the students as they settled into their seats.

As the students settled down, Mr. Rajasekhar greeted them with his usual warm smile. "Namaste, everyone. Today, we are going to explore the beautiful world of Telugu literature, focusing on the works of some of our greatest poets and writers."

He began writing on the board, "Nannaya, Tikkana, and Yerrapragada - The Trinity of Telugu Literature."

"These three poets," he explained, "are known as the 'Kavitrayam' or the trinity of Telugu literature. They played a crucial role in translating the Mahabharata into Telugu, making it accessible to the common people. Let's delve into their contributions and see how they shaped our literary heritage."

The Poets' Contributions

Mr. Rajasekhar started with Nannaya, the first poet of the trinity. "Nannaya Bhattaraka, often called Adi Kavi, began the translation of the Mahabharata from Sanskrit to Telugu. His work not only brought the epic closer to the people but also set the foundation for classical Telugu poetry."

He then moved on to Tikkana. "Tikkana Somayaji continued Nannaya's work, completing many of the unfinished portions. His style was known for its clarity and elegance. He introduced new poetic techniques and made significant contributions to Telugu prosody."

Finally, he spoke about Yerrapragada. "Yerrapragada, also known as Errana, completed the translation of the Mahabharata. His work is celebrated for its depth and richness, capturing the essence of the epic's characters and stories."

Class Discussion

Mr. Rajasekhar encouraged the students to share their thoughts. Shiva raised his hand, "Sir, how did these poets influence the language we speak today?"

"Excellent question, Shiva," Mr. Rajasekhar replied. "Their works laid the foundation for modern Telugu. They standardized the grammar and vocabulary, and their poetic styles influenced generations of writers. Many of the idioms and expressions we use today can be traced back to their works."

Krishna, always curious, asked, "Can you tell us more about their writing styles and how they differed?"

Mr. Rajasekhar smiled, appreciating the interest. "Nannaya's style was formal and scholarly, reflecting his background as a court poet. Tikkana's poetry was more accessible, with a focus on clarity and beauty. Yerrapragada's work combined the best of both, with deep philosophical insights and lyrical elegance."

Group Activity

To make the lesson more engaging, Mr. Raj

The Kingdom of Fools

The next morning, Shiva, Krishna, Ram, Anji, Lakshman, and Abhi were back at school, buzzing with excitement from their recent discoveries. As they settled into their seats for English class, Mr. Mukherji, their teacher, walked in with his common trademark mischievous grin.

The Role Play

"Good morning, class!" Mr. Mukherji greeted, his voice filled with enthusiasm. "Today, we're going to do something a little different. Instead of our usual lesson, we're going to have a role play of 'The Kingdom of Fools.'"

The class perked up, intrigued by the prospect of acting out the story. Mr. Mukherji was known for his wit and humor, and everyone knew this lesson was going to be fun.

Assigning Roles

Mr. Mukherji began assigning roles, his eyes twinkling as he did so. "Shiva, you'll be the king of this peculiar kingdom," he announced. "Krishna, you'll play the role of the wise man who sees through the foolishness."

"Ram, you'll be the royal advisor, and Anji, you'll be the carpenter who gets caught up in the absurdity of the kingdom's rules. Lakshman, you'll be the hapless thief who unwittingly becomes part of the story."

"And Abhi," Mr. Mukherji added with a grin, "you'll be the poor man who ends up entangled in the kingdom's foolish justice system."

The Performance Begins

With roles assigned, the students began their performance. Shiva, as the foolish king, sat on an imaginary throne, trying to look regal while delivering his lines with exaggerated authority. "In this kingdom, day is night, and night is day!" he declared, imitating the absurdity of the kingdom's rules.

Krishna, as the wise man, challenged the king's declarations with a calm and rational demeanor. "But your majesty, this reversal of natural order will only lead to chaos and confusion."

Ram, as the royal advisor, nodded enthusiastically to everything the king said, adding his own absurd suggestions. "Yes, my king! Let us also decree that all people must walk backward to show respect to the sun!"

The Laughter

The class erupted in laughter as the story unfolded, with Anji, playing the carpenter, and Lakshman, as the thief, adding to the humor with their interactions. Abhi's portrayal of the poor man, who found himself unjustly accused and sentenced in the kingdom's bizarre justice system, had everyone in stitches.

Mr. Mukherji watched with delight as his students brought the story to life. His own laughter filled the room as he occasionally interjected with humorous comments, encouraging the students to get even more into their roles.

The Lesson

As the role play came to an end, Mr. Mukherji clapped his hands and praised the class. "Well done, everyone! That was thoroughly entertaining."

He then shifted to a more serious tone. "The story of 'The Kingdom of Fools' is not just about humor, though. It's a satire that teaches us about the dangers of foolish leadership and the importance of wisdom. It reminds us to question absurdity and to value common sense and reason."

Reflection

The students nodded, reflecting on the deeper meaning of the story. Shiva and his friends exchanged glances, thinking about how the lesson applied to their own experiences. The idea of questioning what seemed nonsensical and valuing wisdom resonated with them, especially given the challenges they were beginning to face in their own lives.

The Class Ends

As the bell rang, signaling the end of the class, Mr. Mukherji gave them one last piece of advice with a smile. "Remember, whether in a kingdom of fools or the real world, it's always important to think critically and to act wisely."

The students left the classroom, still chuckling about the role play but also pondering the lesson they had learned. Shiva and his friends, in particular, felt more prepared for the adventures ahead, knowing that they needed to rely not only on their powers but also on their wisdom and critical thinking.

1. The Hidden Temple's Legacy

Chapter 10: The Return to the Temple

After the strange encounter with the shadowy figure, Shiva and his friends decided to revisit the mysterious temple where their adventure began. As they approached the temple, they were greeted by a wise old caretaker who revealed that the temple held ancient secrets and stories waiting to be discovered.

The Caretaker's Revelation

The caretaker, with a long white beard and eyes that seemed to hold the wisdom of the ages, welcomed them warmly. "Welcome back, young adventurers," he said. "I have been expecting you."

Shiva, curious, asked, "Who are you, and how do you know us?"

"I am the guardian of this temple, tasked with protecting its ancient knowledge and guiding those destined to uncover its secrets," the caretaker replied. "This temple is not only a place of worship but also a repository of lost knowledge, with inscriptions that speak of heroes from myths and legends."

Exploring the Temple

Intrigued, the group followed the caretaker deeper into the temple. They passed through corridors adorned with intricate carvings and murals depicting epic battles and divine interventions. The caretaker led them to a hidden chamber, where the walls were covered in ancient inscriptions.

"These inscriptions tell the stories of great heroes and their quests," the caretaker explained. "They speak of courage, wisdom, and the eternal struggle between good and evil."

The Revelation

Krishna, with his keen eye for detail, noticed a series of symbols that resembled the ones they had seen during their transformation. "What do these symbols mean?" he asked.

The caretaker smiled. "These symbols are the marks of the chosen ones, those who are destined to wield the powers of the gods. You, my young friends, are among them. Your adventure has just begun. There are many more secrets to uncover and challenges to face."

Rekindling Curiosity

The discovery rekindled their curiosity and set the stage for future explorations. They realized that their initial adventure was just a glimpse of the temple's vast mysteries. Each inscription and mural held clues to their powers and their purpose.

The Promise of Future Adventures

Before they left, the caretaker gave them a parting gift – a map of the temple, highlighting areas yet to be explored. "Use this map wisely," he said. "It will guide you on your journey and help you uncover the temple's deepest secrets."

With renewed determination, Shiva, Krishna, Ram, Anji, and Lakshman vowed to return and continue their exploration. The temple, with its ancient knowledge and hidden stories, promised many more adventures and the chance to understand their divine powers fully.

As they walked away from the temple, the sun setting behind them, they knew that their journey had only just begun. The mysteries of the temple and their newfound powers awaited them, ready to test their courage and unity once more.

2. The Enigmatic Coin

The Discovery

After their intense day at school, Shiva, Krishna, Ram, Anji, and Lakshman decided to unwind with a small gathering at Abhi's house. The party was lively, with laughter and conversations filling the air. As the night drew to a close and the guests left, the group stayed behind to help Abhi clean up.

The Mysterious Coin

While raking up a pile of leaves in the backyard, Abhi's rake hit something solid. Curious, he bent down and uncovered an old, ornate coin buried under the leaves. The coin was unlike anything they had ever seen, with intricate designs and strange symbols etched into its surface.

"Hey, guys, look at this!" Abhi called out, holding the coin up to the light. The group gathered around, their eyes widening with fascination.

Seeking Answers

Intrigued by the mysterious coin, they decided to show it to Mr. Sharma, the town's old historian. Mr. Sharma was known for his extensive knowledge of ancient artifacts and local legends.

The next day, they visited Mr. Sharma's cluttered office, filled with books, maps, and various historical items. The old historian adjusted his glasses as he examined the coin closely.

"This is a remarkable find," Mr. Sharma said, his voice filled with awe. "This coin is a relic from a bygone era, likely from the ancient kingdom of Harappa. The symbols and designs suggest it may possess mystical properties."

Unveiling the Coin's History

Mr. Sharma explained, "Legend has it that such coins were used by ancient priests to channel divine energies. Each coin was believed to be imbued with the power of the gods, meant to protect and guide those who possess it."

Shiva and his friends exchanged excited glances. The coin's potential connection to their recent transformation at the temple was impossible to ignore.

"Do you think this coin has anything to do with the powers we received?" Krishna asked, his curiosity piqued.

Mr. Sharma nodded thoughtfully. "It's possible. The symbols on this coin are similar to those found in ancient temples dedicated to various deities. This could be a link between your transformation and the ancient knowledge stored within the temple."

The Investigation Begins

The group decided to investigate further. With Mr. Sharma's guidance, they delved into historical texts and maps, trying to uncover more about the coin's origins and its connection to their powers.

Their research led them to discover that the coin was part of a set of ancient artifacts, each with unique properties. These artifacts were scattered across different sacred sites, and together, they formed a key to unlocking even greater mysteries.

Preparing for the Journey

Equipped with new knowledge and a sense of purpose, Shiva, Krishna, Ram, Anji, Lakshman, and Abhi prepared for their next adventure. They knew that finding the remaining artifacts and understanding their powers was crucial in protecting their world from any future threats.

The Adventure Continues

As they embarked on their quest, they couldn't help but feel a sense of excitement and anticipation. The discovery of the coin had reignited their curiosity and determination. With the ancient artifact in hand and the guidance of Mr. Sharma, they were ready to uncover the secrets of the past and embrace their destiny as modern-day heroes.

The journey ahead promised challenges and revelations, but with their unity and newfound powers, they were prepared to face whatever lay ahead. The mysterious coin was just the beginning, a key to unlocking the ancient knowledge that would guide them in their ongoing battle against darkness.

The Legend Of The Lost City

As part of their school research project, Shiva, Krishna, Ram, Anji, Lakshman, and Abhi spent hours in the library, poring over old books and manuscripts. One day, while sifting through dusty volumes, they stumbled upon a fascinating legend: a tale of a lost city rumored to be hidden deep in the forest nearby.

The Legend Unveiled

The legend spoke of a magnificent city, once thriving but now forgotten, buried under centuries of foliage and mystery. According to the ancient texts, the city was protected by ancient spirits and held untold treasures, both material and mystical. The story detailed how the city was a center of learning and spiritual power, attracting sages and warriors from far and wide.

Krishna, always the avid reader, read aloud from one of the manuscripts, "The lost city, known as Hiranyagarbha, is said to be guarded by spirits of the past. Only those pure of heart and brave of spirit can uncover its secrets and harness its power."

The Excitement Builds

The story of Hiranyagarbha captivated the group. It seemed to resonate with their recent adventures and the mysteries they had begun to unravel.

"This could be the adventure we've been waiting for," Ram said, his eyes gleaming with excitement. "Imagine what we could discover there!"

Shiva nodded, "And the connection to ancient spirits and treasures might help us understand our own powers better."

Planning the Trek

Determined to uncover the truth behind the legend, the friends began planning their trek to the forest. They gathered maps, survival gear, and anything they thought might help them on their journey. Mr. Sharma, the town historian who had previously helped them, provided additional insights and warned them about the potential dangers they might face.

"The forest is dense and filled with wildlife," Mr. Sharma cautioned. "But if the legend is true, what you find there could be invaluable. Trust each other and stay safe."

Setting Off

One bright Saturday morning, the group set off for the forest, filled with anticipation and a sense of adventure. As they trekked deeper into the woods, the trees grew taller and the underbrush thicker. The air was filled with the sounds of birds and rustling leaves, creating an atmosphere of both serenity and mystery.

The Journey Begins

Guided by their map and the descriptions from the manuscripts, they made their way through the forest, keeping an eye out for any signs of the lost city. Hours turned into days as they navigated the challenging terrain, but their determination never wavered.

Lakshman, using his keen sense of direction, led the way, while Anji's strength came in handy when they needed to clear paths or climb obstacles. Abhi, with his quick thinking, devised solutions to the various challenges they encountered, and Krishna's knowledge provided valuable insights into the historical clues they found along the way.

The First Glimpse

On the third day of their journey, just as the sun began to set, they stumbled upon an ancient stone pathway, overgrown with vines and moss. The path seemed to lead deeper into the forest, towards a place where the trees parted to reveal a faint, ethereal glow.

"This must be it," Shiva said, his voice filled with awe. "The entrance to Hiranyagarbha."

One night, as Shiva was studying, he heard a knock at the door. To his surprise, an old courier stood there, holding a parchment sealed with wax. The courier handed it to him without a word and left into the night.

The Cryptic Message

Shiva carefully broke the seal and unrolled the parchment. The message was written in elegant, flowing script:

"To the Seekers of Truth,

You are cordially invited to a secret gathering of individuals with a profound interest in mythology and the supernatural. Your recent experiences have not gone unnoticed. Join us at midnight at the old mansion on Maple Street.

- The Order of the Ancient Ones"

Shiva's heart raced as he read the message. He immediately called his friends, who arrived at his house without hesitation. Together, they examined the invitation, their excitement palpable.

The Gathering

At midnight, they arrived at the old mansion on Maple Street, its grandeur shadowed by age and mystery. The door creaked open as they approached, and a figure in a hooded cloak gestured for them to enter.

Inside, the mansion was filled with scholars, historians, and enthusiasts, all animatedly discussing various myths and supernatural phenomena. The walls were lined with ancient books, relics, and artifacts from different cultures.

Meeting the Order

A distinguished-looking man approached the group, introducing himself as Professor Arya, the leader of the Order of the Ancient Ones. "Welcome, young seekers," he greeted. "We've been expecting you."

Shiva and his friends introduced themselves and shared their recent experiences at the temple and with the mysterious coin.

Professor Arya listened intently, his eyes widening with interest.

"This is remarkable," he said. "Your encounters align with many ancient prophecies and myths we have studied. The powers you've gained and the artifacts you've found are part of a larger tapestry of ancient knowledge."

New Insights

Throughout the night, the group mingled with scholars who provided new insights into their experiences. One scholar, Dr. Patel, explained the significance of the symbols on the coin. "These symbols are ancient runes, often used in rituals to invoke divine protection and power. Your discovery of the coin is no coincidence."

Another enthusiast, Ms. Rao, shared legends of other individuals who had been granted divine powers in times of great need. "You are part of an ancient lineage of heroes," she said. "Your powers are meant to protect and restore balance."

The Connection

Krishna, always inquisitive, asked, "How do we control and harness these powers to their full potential?"

Professor Arya replied, "Understanding the origins of your powers and the artifacts you possess is key. The temple you discovered is one of many nodes of ancient energy. Studying these sites and their histories will help you unlock your full potential."

The Journey Ahead

As the gathering came to an end, the friends felt a renewed sense of purpose and determination. The Order of the Ancient Ones had provided them with valuable knowledge and a network of allies.

Before they left, Professor Arya handed them a book filled with ancient texts and maps. "Use this to guide you on your journey," he said. "The path ahead is fraught with challenges, but with knowledge and unity, you will prevail."

Embracing Their Destiny

Leaving the mansion, the friends walked into the night, their minds buzzing with new information and ideas. The secret gathering had opened their eyes to the vast world of mythology and the supernatural, and they were eager to explore it further.

With their newfound knowledge and the support of the Order, Shiva, Krishna, Ram, Anji, Lakshman, and Abhi were ready to embrace their destiny. Their journey was just beginning, and they were prepared to face whatever challenges lay ahead, armed with the wisdom of the ancients and the strength of their bond.

The Unsolved Puzzle

Saraswati discovered an ancient puzzle in an old library book while researching Hindu scriptures. The puzzle, once solved, was believed to reveal the location of hidden wisdom and artifacts from ancient times. The friends took on the challenge, working together to decode the clues and unlock the secrets hidden within the puzzle.

The Whispering Forest

The friends decided to explore the forest where they had heard strange whispers during their encounter with the shadowy figure. As they ventured deeper, they discovered an ancient grove with trees that seemed to whisper ancient chants and tales. The grove held remnants of rituals and artifacts that offered clues about their mysterious experience and hinted at further adventures.

As the young warriors returned to their routine, a sense of unease from their encounter with the dark presence lingered. They realized the importance of not only honing their physical abilities but also strengthening their minds and spirits. Thus, they embarked on a journey of daily meditation and spiritual practice to cultivate inner strength and resilience.

Each morning, as the first light of dawn crept over the horizon, the group gathered in the tranquil garden of their school, a serene spot they had chosen for their meditative practices.

Shiva, with his unwavering focus, sat cross-legged under a large peepal tree. Eyes closed and heart centered, he chanted the **Maha Mrityunjaya Mantra**. The powerful vibrations of the mantra resonated through his being, invoking the blessings of Lord Shiva and the healing energy to overcome fear and adversity.And he is also reading *shiv purana* as well as balancing his studies.

Krishna, always radiant and full of energy, found solace in listening to the **Shri Hari Stotram**. The melodious verses filled the air, celebrating the glory of Lord Vishnu. The rhythmic chants soothed his mind and brought a sense of peace, reminding him of the divine protection that surrounded them.

Anji, dedicated and devout, read the **Hanuman Chalisa** every day. His voice echoed with devotion as he recited the verses that praised the virtues and heroic deeds of Lord Hanuman. With each chant, he felt the strength and courage of Hanuman infusing his spirit, preparing him to face any challenge with unwavering determination.

Ram, the epitome of righteousness, listened to the repetitive and calming chant of **Shri Ram Ram Rameti.** The simplicity and purity of the chant reflected his own values and principles, reinforcing his commitment to dharma. Lakshman, ever loyal to his brother, joined Ram in this practice, finding harmony and unity in their shared devotion.

Saraswati, the embodiment of wisdom, chanted the **Gayatri Mantra.** Her voice, clear and pure, invoked the divine light of knowledge and wisdom. The mantra, a prayer to the sun deity, filled her with a sense of clarity and purpose, guiding her in her quest for learning and understanding.

Arjun, disciplined and introspective, surprised everyone by joining Karna each day to read the **SrimadBhagavad Gita.** The ancient scripture, a dialogue between Lord Krishna and Arjuna, offered profound insights into life, duty, and righteousness. As they read and discussed the verses, both Arjun and Karna found new perspectives and deepened their understanding of their paths.

The garden became a sanctuary of tranquility and spiritual growth. The diverse practices of each warrior created a symphony of devotion and meditation, blending together in perfect harmony. The air was thick with the sacred energy of their chants, resonating with the power of their collective intentions.

Through these daily practices, the young warriors experienced profound transformations. They found balance and clarity, their minds becoming as sharp as their skills. The spiritual strength they cultivated allowed them to approach their challenges with renewed vigor and confidence. They realized that true power lay not just in their abilities but also in their inner resilience and connection to the divine.

The bond between them grew stronger, united by their shared journey of self-improvement. They supported and inspired each other, learning from their individual practices and experiences. The garden became a place of learning, reflection, and growth, nurturing their spirits and preparing them for the battles ahead.

As they continued their meditation and spiritual practices, the young warriors felt a sense of calm and purpose. They knew that whatever challenges lay ahead, they were ready to face them with unwavering strength and unwavering faith.

The Author's Note

1. Reflection and Gratitude

As we close the first chapter of this extraordinary journey, I want to express my deepest gratitude to every reader who has joined us. Your enthusiasm and support have been the driving forces behind this story. The characters and their adventures are a testament to the power of imagination and the joy of storytelling. Thank you for embarking on this journey with us, and I hope you've enjoyed every moment as much as I have enjoyed crafting it.

2. Acknowledgments

I extend my heartfelt thanks to everyone who contributed to the creation of this story. To my friends and family, whose encouragement and feedback were invaluable; to the mentors and scholars who inspired me with their wisdom; and to the countless authors and creators whose work has shaped my understanding of storytelling—this story would not have been possible without you. Your support and inspiration are deeply appreciated.

3. A Special Thanks

A special thank you goes to my fellow enthusiasts of mythology, cricket, and anime. Your passion and dedication have been a source of inspiration. Your conversations and insights have greatly influenced the development of this narrative, and for that, I am truly grateful.

4. Invitation to Continue the Journey

As we conclude this part of our story, I invite you to stay tuned for the next chapters of this adventure. The journey is far from over, and there are many more twists, turns, and discoveries awaiting. Your continued engagement and curiosity will be the keys to unlocking the next phases of our tale.

5. Behind the Scenes

Creating this story has been a labor of love, and I am excited to share a glimpse behind the scenes. From brainstorming sessions and character development to the intricacies of plot weaving, each step has been a fascinating journey. I hope this glimpse into the creative process adds to your enjoyment of the story.

6. Reader's Reflections

I encourage you to reflect on the themes and characters introduced in this part of the story. What resonated with you? How did the adventures and mythological elements influence your thoughts? Sharing your reflections and interpretations can be a wonderful way to engage with the story on a deeper level.

7. Feedback and Interaction

Your feedback is invaluable. If you have any thoughts, comments, or suggestions, I would love to hear from you. Your insights can help shape future installments and ensure that the story continues to evolve in exciting and meaningful ways.

8. Next Steps

With the conclusion of this part, the stage is set for new adventures and deeper explorations. Keep an eye out for the next chapters, where the characters will face new challenges, uncover hidden truths, and continue their journey of discovery. The best is yet to come.

9. A Note on Mythology and Fiction

The blend of mythological elements with fictional storytelling is a passion of mine. It allows us to explore timeless themes and engage with ancient wisdom in a contemporary context. I hope this story has sparked your interest in these fascinating intersections and encouraged you to explore further.

10. Farewell for Now

As we wrap up this part of the story, I want to extend a warm farewell for now. May the adventures and characters we've encountered stay with you, and may you carry their lessons and experiences into your own life. Until we meet again in the next chapter, thank you for being part of this journey.

Part Two: "The Guardians Of Divinity: Shadows Of The Past"

As the sun rose higher, casting a golden hue over the village, Shiva, Krishna, Ram, Anji, Lakshman, Saraswati and Abhi stood together, united by fate and a shared purpose. Their journey was just beginning, each step a testament to their courage and friendship. With Saraswati's wisdom now guiding them, they felt stronger and more prepared for the battles ahead.

But as they looked towards the horizon, they knew the world held many more mysteries and dangers. With their divine powers and unwavering bond, they were ready to face whatever came their way. Their adventure in the temple was just the first chapter of a much larger story, one filled with challenges, discoveries, and the unbreakable spirit of true heroes.

To Be Continued...

Next Part: "The Guardians of Divinity: Shadows of the Past"

In the next installment, the young warriors are called to a distant land where ancient secrets and forgotten legends await. As they uncover the mysteries of their powers, they will face new enemies and forge new alliances. The fate of the world once again hangs in the balance, and only the Guardians of Divinity can save it. Join Shiva, Krishna, Ram, Anji, Lakshman, and Saraswati as they embark on a new adventure, where the shadows of the past threaten to engulf the present. Will they triumph over the darkness, or will the ancient evil finally prevail? The journey continues...

To Be Continued................

Epilogue: Shadows of the Past

As the last rays of sunlight faded into the horizon, the group sat in their favorite spot in the park, basking in the peace they had worked so hard to achieve. Hyderabad thrived around them, free from the shadows that had once loomed over it. Laughter filled the air, and for a moment, everything seemed perfect.

But as night fell, a sense of unease settled over the group. Shiva, ever the vigilant leader, felt it first—a subtle shift in the air, a whisper of something long forgotten. He glanced at his friends, and from their expressions, he knew they felt it too."Did you feel that?" Saraswati asked, her voice barely above a whisper.Krishna nodded, his eyes narrowing as he scanned the darkening sky. "Something's not right."

Anju, usually full of energy and optimism, looked uncharacteristically serious. "It's like before, but different. Older. More... sinister."Lakshman, always the strategist, frowned. "We need to find out what it is. We can't let our guard down."As they discussed the strange occurrence, a cold wind swept through the park, carrying with it the faint sound of ancient chants. The ground beneath them seemed to tremble, and shadows danced unnaturally at the edge of their vision.Suddenly, a bright flash illuminated the night sky, followed by a thunderous roar. The group jumped to their feet, their hearts pounding with a mix of fear and determination. From the depths of the shadows, a figure emerged—a hooded figure, eyes glowing with a malevolent light."I am the Keeper of Secrets," the figure intoned, his voice echoing with a chilling resonance. "You have defeated Kaal, but his power was but a fragment of a far greater darkness. The past is never truly gone, and the shadows of ancient times have returned to reclaim what was lost."The figure vanished as quickly as he had appeared, leaving the group in stunned silence. The air crackled with residual energy, and the sense of impending doom lingered long after the figure had gone.Ram broke the silence. "We need to prepare. Whatever this is, it's coming for us."Saraswati nodded, her resolve hardening. "We'll face it together, just as we always have."As the group gathered their thoughts and steeled their resolve, they knew that their next journey would be even more perilous. The shadows of the past had awakened, and the Guardians of Divinity would once again be called to protect their world from an ancient evil that threatened to consume it.

Coming Soon: The Guardians of Divinity: Shadows of the Past

Prepare for an epic adventure as Shiva, Krishna, Ram, Anju, Lakshman, Saraswati, Arjuna, and Karna delve into the mysteries of their heritage, uncover long-forgotten secrets, and face a darkness older and more powerful than they ever imagined. The battle between light and shadow continues, and the fate of their world hangs in the balance.